# BLOOD PAWN

SIERRA ROWAN

# JOIN SIERRA ROWAN'S INSIDER'S CLUB

For the latest book updates, sales, giveaways, and more, join Sierra Rowan's Insiders Club at sierrarowan.com/subscribe!

# AUTHOR'S NOTE

If you would like content guidance, please see the author's website at sierrarowan.com.

# PROLOGUE
## WREN

"Tell us what happened, Wren."

Handcuffs glinted beneath the bright lights and rested like anchors on my wrists. I couldn't feel my feet anymore. My legs either, courtesy of the hard plastic chair slowly cutting off whatever remained of my circulation. The metal table was glued to my wrists, and nothing was like the old cop dramas Harper had loved so much. There was no dark room. No cop leaning against the wall in the corner, smoking a cigarette or chewing a toothpick or whatever it was they did on those shows. Everything was bright. Recorded. Catalogued for future reference.

Not that I'd ever make it to a trial.

"We can't help you if you won't help us."

Dried sweat made my fingers feel gritty, and dirt did too. Cemetery mud formed dark half-moons beneath my nails.

"Wren, please."

I tensed at the sound of my mother's voice from beside me, and guilt like a dull knife began sawing its way through my chest again. It was my fault. All of it. I'd trade places if I could.

"Honey, just tell us the truth."

I squeezed my eyes shut against hot tears I couldn't let myself shed, and the chemical stink of cologne wafted into the air when the detective stepped away from me. His small huff of frustration was loud to my ears.

"Dammit, girl," he muttered.

The table quivered. I opened my eyes to find him on the other side, his fists bracing him as he looked down at me. His blue eyes were exasperated, and somewhere along the line, he'd loosened his brown-and-green-checkered tie. A tuft of his short blond hair stood on end. The rest hadn't shifted position in hours.

"Come on, Wren." He shook his head at me. "Just tell us why you killed your sister."

**1**

———

WREN

*Five Days Earlier*

"I swear to God," Harper announced, flopping down between Brayden and me on the log bench. "If Trent Pilson hits on me *one more time* tonight, I'm going to break his nose. I don't care if he's the quarterback. He's done."

Barely keeping myself from spitting out my soda with a startled laugh, I glanced at my sister, the track star, theater star, and pretty-much-everything-else star of Claremont College, not to mention current vice president of her sorority. My fraternal twin and I had precious little in common in that regard—besides our hazel eyes, we didn't even look similar—but she was still the closest person to me in the world. An irritated expression on her face, she leaned back, her arms bracing her on the rough log. Bonfire light from the enormous blaze fifty yards away danced across her waves of blond hair and lit up her striped tank top and pale shorts. Stretching out her legs and balancing one foot atop the other, she rolled her head to the side, regarding Brayden and me both. "You think Dad would mind if I did?"

"His daughter breaking the nose of his boss's son?" I scoffed. "No, I can't imagine why he'd see that as a problem."

Harper sighed, tilting her head back. "You sure? Mom would probably applaud me."

"For assault and battery? Doubtful."

"Shame."

"Not really."

She rocked to the side, bumping her shoulder into mine, a smirk tugging at her lip. "Pacifist."

"Tyrant."

Brayden shook his head. His fingers pinched the straw to his soda can, holding it close to his lips. "You two are ridiculous, you know that, right?"

I grinned at the guy who'd been one of my best friends since kindergarten. "You know you love us."

"Mm-hmm, sure." Despite his sarcastic tone, his eyes twinkled with amusement. "And how much longer do I have to stay here, proving my undying affection?"

"Eternity," Harper and I answered in sync.

He chuckled and took a sip of his soda.

"What're you both doing over here, anyhow? Party's that way." Harper notched her head toward the massive bonfire occupying the shore of the river. Silhouetted against the blaze, the population of nearly every Greek house on campus danced or shouted at each other, their words unintelligible over the music blasting from the stereo somewhere in the center of the melee. On the fringes, the unaffiliated students clustered like kids at the edge of a swimming pool, debating whether to risk drowning by jumping in. Firelight played over the leaf canopy above them, while the brilliant full moon lit up the wide river in a silver display.

"Coming with you for moral support does not mean subjecting myself to tedious co-ed hormones," Brayden replied, setting his drink aside. "And that monotonous excuse for music makes me want to go all Phineas Gage and drive a railroad spike through my head."

"Uh-huh." Harper glanced at me. "So, what's your excuse?"

I nodded to my brand-new Converse shoes resting by the log. "Blisters. And pretty much what Brayden said—minus the railroad spike." I gave him a pointed look, which he returned with a grin.

Harper scoffed. "And *you* two are hopeless."

"Victims of good taste," Brayden corrected. "You should try finding some."

"Ha! Is that what you call it?"

"I'll have you know that Chopin's—"

"Oh, God, not Chopin again. You know we're not all music majors here, right?"

Brayden made an affronted noise. I buried a grin and caught Harper doing the same.

"So, where's Ollie?" My sister glanced around.

"Oh, you know..." Brayden drawled.

At Harper's curious look, I twitched my head to the woods behind us. Beyond the shield of the undergrowth, the forest was a black pit. I knew there were trails winding through it—we'd all hiked that hilly terrain plenty of times over the years—but in the darkness, everything was an abyss. "She's, uh—"

A rustling sound interrupted me, and Ollie emerged from the woods with her girlfriend, Emma, only a step behind. At nearly six feet tall, Ollie was a candidate for just about any basketball or volleyball team that wanted her, which meant she'd gotten a full-ride scholarship to Claremont. Her long brown hair was lashed up in her standard ponytail, though it looked a bit disheveled now, and her blouse had a stain on the sleeve where she might've bumped into a tree in the dark. A few inches shorter, with brunette curls that made her look like a human-sized doll, Emma otherwise appeared much the same as Ollie, at least where the disheveling was concerned.

At the sight of Harper, an embarrassed grin flickered over Ollie's face. "Oh, hey."

"Hey," my sister replied dryly.

"You, uh, you enjoying the party?"

"Probably not as much as you two."

Emma ducked her head, even the firelight unable to disguise how red her cheeks turned. Following Ollie, she sank down onto the log across from Brayden, still holding the other girl's hand. "So, um, did Trent Pilson find you—"

Harper groaned loudly. Emma hesitated, casting a nervous glance at the rest of us.

"He's been obsessed with her since freshmen year," Ollie explained. "It's kind of a thing."

"*Not* a thing," Harper and I said at the exact same moment.

Emma eyed us both.

"Not a thing," Harper repeated.

"It's totally a thing," Brayden assured Emma.

Harper snatched a pebble from the ground and tossed it at him. He ducked away with an offended cry. I grinned at them both.

"So," Ollie began, "Emma and I were thinking of heading over to Joe's Diner in a bit, if any of you want to come? Maybe grab some late-night pancakes or—"

A loud, electronic chirp-chirp interrupted her, and bright white headlights suddenly blasted the shore from beyond the party, silhouetting all the college students now frozen in alarm. Red and blue lights flared to life above the glare, and a moment later, the shifting light revealed three cop cars negotiating the narrow road down the slope toward the river.

"Oh, crap," Ollie muttered.

By the bonfire, the stereo cut off sharply. Half the partiers scattered like mice, tearing toward the relative safety of the forest and the cars parked in the lot beyond the trails, while the others gave cries of futile protest.

"Well, kids." Brayden rose to his feet quickly, brushing off his plaid shorts. "Time to go."

Harper motioned for him to stay. "I'm sure it's fine. Probably some fisherman just being a jerk and—"

"And none of us are twenty-one," Ollie called, already by the edge of the forest with Emma. "What do you think the cops'll say when they see the beer cans all over this place?"

My sister and I shared a brief look. "Mom might be with them," I said.

Harper shot up from the log and started after Brayden. "Let's go."

I shoved my feet into my shoes as the sound of car doors slamming came from up ahead. I glanced up, tying my laces on autopilot. The cops climbed from their vehicles, taking off across the gravel beach toward the people trying to escape. Flashlight beams pierced the fire-lit night, sweeping and bobbing wildly across the fleeing partiers.

"Wren, come on!" Harper urged, waving a hand at me from the edge of the woods.

I rushed after her, darting past the cover of the trees with her only a few steps ahead. With a quick look back, she tossed me a nervous grin in the last edges of the firelight that stretched past the trees.

I returned it, though the expression turned to a wince a heartbeat later when I started walking. I hadn't been joking about the blisters. I loved these shoes, *had* loved them since I bought them last weekend at the mall, but little had I known when I headed out this evening that the things liked to chew on my ankles like rabid Chihuahuas.

Much more of this, and I'd be bleeding.

"This way," Ollie called in a low voice from up ahead.

We all started after her through the undergrowth. The glow of the firelight cast long, dwindling shadows from the tree trunks and picked out what I hoped was a trail climbing up the slope away from the beach. Boulders and fallen logs lay scattered amid the bushes and weeds like a natural obstacle course, blocking even the thin track through the woods. I vaguely remembered the trail from a hike a few months ago, but the knowledge did me little good. Not when, after only a dozen yards, the last traces of the firelight were gone, swallowed by darkness.

"Anyone know where we're going?" I whispered, glancing around nervously. The more my eyes adjusted, the more I thought maybe I could make out a trace of moonlight to my left, where the trees thinned at the cliff's edge.

"Yeah, kinda," Ollie replied, following the winding path as it curved that way. "The trail leads—"

She cut off with an oomph and a sudden rustle of undergrowth.

I stopped cold. "Ollie, you okay?"

"Yeah." She sounded aggrieved, and more rustling sounds followed. "Fine."

A white light flared to life ahead of me. I winced, my eyes stinging. "What the—"

Brayden gave me a questioning look, his cell phone clutched in his hand and its flashlight glaring like a lighthouse in the darkness. In the glow, Ollie was clambering to her feet with Emma's help. At my side, Harper held up a hand, trying to block the light from reaching her eyes.

"Turn that off, you idiot!" Ollie hissed, brushing leaves from her legs. "You want the cops finding us?"

"Idiot? You just fell. We need light to—"

"I said turn it *off*."

Brayden frowned. The forest plunged back into darkness.

"There's a break in the woods at the top of the hill," Emma said.

"Okay," Brayden allowed, "but if no one can see, how are we going to get there?"

Silence followed.

"Fine," Ollie grumbled. "But keep the beam aimed at the ground, okay?"

The flashlight flared to life again. Scowling, Ollie resumed leading the way up the hill, Emma and the others right behind her.

I cast a glance over my shoulder. What little I could see of the river shore beyond the trees seemed empty of anyone but cops now, and none of the police were heading toward us on the hillside. A new siren announced a fire truck somewhere in the distance, probably sent to put the bonfire out, but thus far, the blaze still burned, lighting up the beach and the cops so well that we would be easily able to see anyone coming after us.

A breath left me, and I hurried after the others. The trail climbed up to trace along the edge of the cliff, and at its highest point, a log fence bordered it, separating us from the abyss. But if I remembered correctly, at the bottom of the hill, the trail turned and climbed back toward the parking lot.

This might work. If we made it to our cars before the cops, Mom might never know we—

Something slammed into my right side, knocking me hard toward the cliff. I crashed into the fence, but it didn't stop me. My body tumbled past the barrier, and only the fact my arms instinctively wrapped around the top log kept me from falling all the way down.

The dark drop toward the river loomed beneath me, a hundred feet straight into the black water.

Rough wood cut into me as I clung to the beam, making pain flare hot across my palms and forearms. My feet scrambled for purchase on the rocky cliff face, and over the blood rushing in my ears, I could hear my friends shouting and running back down the trail toward me.

I couldn't look away from the plummet to certain death.

"Grab her!" Harper cried.

"Oh my God, Wren." From the corner of my eyes, I spotted Brayden reaching for me. "Just don't move."

I choked on a scoff. Like I was going to—

Wood cracked. The log lurched.

My sister's shocked face was the last thing I saw before I tumbled over the cliff.

**2**

---

ASHER

ine hundred and twenty-three years, and I still couldn't stand the feeling of bugs crawling on me during a hunt.

"You *sure* the dormants told you they saw signs of them here?" Ulysses muttered, his voice in my earpiece so low even I could barely hear it.

Gideon made an irritated sound over the mics. "As I have repeated ten times already, *yes*."

"Because we've been here for hours, and all *I've* seen is a raccoon trying to eat my face and a pair of coyotes getting it on in the—"

"Quiet," I whispered.

The others fell silent. I buried a grimace and resisted the urge to swat away the spider who, by now, had probably laid eggs on my shirt.

Gods below, I despised bugs.

"We *could* try somewhere else," Liam whispered, the sound of rushing water undercutting the dry rasp of his damaged voice. Two hundred yards downriver, he lay beneath bushes only a short distance from the shore. "They may have left."

The others were silent, waiting.

I fought back a sigh, studying the terrain on the opposite side of the river from my own spot within a tangle of undergrowth. Like the cliff on which I lay, the landscape across from me ended in a rocky, near-vertical drop straight into the water below. About a half-mile to the right of that, the hillside sloped down to a beach, and from the firelight and music, I could guess the locals were having some sort of party. To the left, the rolling hills of the forest preserve seemed occupied only by nocturnal creatures, while the idly curving river swept past, fast but deep and touched with silver by the moonlit sky. Everything was peaceful. Motionless. And the raucous group of locals were too large a target to be appealing.

Rabids wouldn't stay long in a place like this.

I frowned. If the dormants said they saw signs of those bastards, then I was loath to leave, especially since the thick woods and dark caves around us made for a decent place to spend the day. But Ulysses and Liam also had a point. A pack of rabids could have easily moved on by now. Regardless, barring the locals on the beach, there weren't likely to be too many people around after sundown.

Not the best hunting grounds.

"Where would they go?" I murmured. "What's close by?"

"Besides the town?" Gideon was quiet for a moment. "A park service building one mile west of my position, a few tourist traps beyond that, and a public park two miles south, all likely to be closed after sunset. There *is* the bar about a mile beyond the park, and you know Laz doesn't like to take sides if he can avoid—"

The bleep-chirp noise of a police car came from the west, cutting him off. My attention slid to the side, and my eyes tracked the flashing lights painting red and blue across the trees and water alike. So much for the party, then.

I returned my attention to the landscape while the others waited in silence. Moving before the police cleared out would just be foolish, and that was assuming we moved at all. If the rabids *were* here, with the humans gone they might be more inclined to leave wherever they were hiding.

Seconds turned to minutes while bats swooped over the trees and the river rushed past. The spinning lights remained where they were, though far in the distance a fire engine howled a warning as if planning to join them soon. The spider made its way past the neckline of my shirt and started down my spine. I closed my eyes, cursing silently.

"Any sign they've encroached on the city yet?" I whispered, forcing myself back to my study of the terrain.

"None of the dormants mentioned anything," Ulysses replied.

My mouth tightened. That didn't necessarily mean the rabids *hadn't* made forays into town. After centuries of dwindling numbers, the rabid population had been on the increase these past few decades, making them bolder and more dangerous than ever. Admittedly, dormants were usually pretty good about keeping us apprised of any infiltration—the last thing anyone needed were a bunch of those vicious bastards drawing attention to themselves and bringing the government down on our heads—but they were still civilians. They might have missed something.

A light flared in the forest. My focus darted toward the bright beam piercing the dark woods in time to see a girl climbing to her feet with the help of another.

The light vanished. Unbothered, I studied the five figures in the shadows, my night vision easily picking them out in shimmering lines of silver. They didn't move like rabids and from what I could determine over the distance, they didn't feel like them either.

My lip twitched. Partiers, then. Probably trying to get away before the cops found them.

The beam flared to life again, aimed at the ground this time. The group started up the slope, walking slowly like a bunch of humans trying to find their way through the darkness.

Which had to be exactly what they were, considering rabids wouldn't need a flashlight.

My eyes trailed them for a few moments before returning to the dark terrain.

"Bar sounds like the best bet," I whispered.

Ulysses made a small noise of agreement.

"Okay." I glanced toward the fire and the cops. "We'll give it another hour and then head for the—"

A scream cut through the night.

My attention snapped back in time to see a black blur rip past a dark-haired girl at the rear of the group and then fly onward across the cliff-face like a shadow come to life. The girl herself clung to the log railing while her friends shouted and raced toward her.

They weren't fast enough.

The log cracked. The girl tumbled over the edge of the cliff toward the rapids below.

A shadow snagged her before she made it twenty feet.

"*Shit!*" Ulysses swore over my earpiece.

The black blur wrapped around the dark-haired young woman, engulfing her like a blanket, before taking off toward the east. To her screaming friends she'd simply look like she vanished into the darkness.

"Move!" I ordered, shoving up from beneath the undergrowth.

Rustling came over my earpiece. The others, hurrying to obey.

But we were falling behind. Losing sight of the shadow and in it, the girl. The bastard was already a mile or more ahead, moving like it knew someone would be chasing it.

"Dammit," I growled.

I dove over the edge of the cliff.

**3**

———

WREN

Darkness swallowed me, and something muffled my scream like a hand over my face.

But the river never came.

Gravity yanked me around like I was on a roller coaster, and the wind howled in my ears. I swore I heard laughter—dark and male and cruel—coming from every-where, but I couldn't see anyone, and no matter how I thrashed and fought, nothing changed.

Something hard slammed into my side, and then the darkness ripped away like a curtain yanked off of my face.

I was on the ground, lying in a patch of moonlight. The river rushed by only a few yards ahead, and rocky cliff walls rose on either side of me and behind. Wet gravel and sand lay beneath me, not covered in my blood. Not the last thing I saw before I died.

My heart pounding, I gaped at the tiny cove. I was alive. Not broken and bleeding on the ground—my cut hands and blistered ankles aside.

How was I alive?

A shadow passed in front of me and then... shifted. Rippled like fabric and then drew down and back in on itself, somehow transitioning seamlessly from a nebulous blur of darkness into the form of a man with ragged hair and a ripped trench coat, crouching in the moonlight at the water's edge.

Grinning at me.

"Hi, pretty." He dragged out the words around his rotted teeth.

Shaking spread through me, like my body couldn't keep up with the sheer fact that *couldn't* have just happened. What I'd just seen wasn't possible. Wasn't real.

Three more shadows rippled and changed near the water, shifting from darkness into other men. Ragged clothes covered them, stained and torn and filthy, like a stench transformed into fabric. The shortest of the trio leered at me, his hungry grin making me want to retreat through the rock if only to get away from him. The tallest man turned, glaring at the river and the cliffs like he expected them to sprout enemies.

"Get up there," he snapped at the two others alongside him. "Keep watch."

The shortest man made a complaining noise. "No fun. I like it when they're scared."

"I thought I might've seen something back there."

The short guy growled as if irritated, but he jumped up, scaling the rough rock walls like an acrobat and then disappearing over the cliff's edge, and the other guy with him followed. The man closest to me chuckled, contempt thick in the sound, and then shuffled toward where I lay, never leaving his crouched position.

I kicked at his face the moment he came within reach.

His hand lashed out, catching my ankle and yanking me off-balance. Frantically, I swung with my other foot, and my shoe connected with his chest. His grip fell from my ankle.

I scrambled backward, my bleeding palms shoving at the wet gravel until the cliff wall stopped me. There wasn't any way past the men. Any way up the wall.

Maybe we weren't too far from the cops.

"Help!" I screamed. "Somebody help—"

With a snarl like a wild animal, the squat man rushed at me, grabbing me and shoving me back against the rocks. "Shut it," he growled.

My eyes stung at the putrid odor of rotted meat and sewage coming off his clothes, and bile rose in the back of my throat, choking me. I turned my face aside, pushing back at the stone behind me like maybe, maybe it would let me through.

From the corner of my eye, I saw his lips curl in another grin, and horror spread through me. His teeth. Something was wrong with those nasty, stained teeth. They weren't—

So fast, I could barely see him move, his hand whipped out and snagged my wrist, yanking it toward him and sending me toppling to the ground. With a grip like a vise, he wrenched my hand up toward his face.

"Mmm..." His tongue stretched out, and he raked it across the bloody cuts on my palm, ignoring how I struggled to pull away. "Yummy, yummy, y—"

He blinked, his gleeful expression falling away and becoming alarmed. His eyes went from my hand to my face, and then his tongue lashed out a second time, whipping across my wounds swiftly. Without looking away from me, he snapped something to the tall man in a language I'd never heard.

The guy gaped at him like he'd lost his mind.

I swung my free hand hard, aiming a punch at the crouching man's face.

He snagged that wrist too, snarling again, and wrenched my shoulder. Pain blinded me. It felt like my arm had been torn off. Through the haze, I heard him bark unintelligible words at the other man, his voice insistent and aggravated.

"Please," I gasped. "Just let me go. I won't—"

The tall man strode across the cove, practically shoving the crouched guy out of the way. Snatching my arm, he yanked me upright, and I shrieked as agony radiated from my shoulder.

For a moment, he simply glared at me like I'd done something horrible. His dark eyes raked over my face like he couldn't believe what he was seeing.

"Please..." I begged. "Just let me—"

Whipping me around so fast that I stumbled, he grabbed my hair, yanking my head to the side.

Pain pierced my neck like someone had just jabbed knives straight into my throat. I opened my mouth, but instantly his hand clamped down, trapping my scream.

A sucking sensation pulled at my skin. My thoughts blurred, swirling like I was falling down a dark tunnel through my own body and into his. My God, he was swallowing my—

The knife-feeling ripped away, and he spun me around to face him again as the world swum back into surreal focus. His voice aghast, the tall man said something to the other guy, all while staring at me like I'd suddenly sprouted two heads. Blood—*my* blood—coated his chin like glistening paint. Shaking, I pressed my free hand to my neck, finding my skin wet and sticky, and tears burned my eyes as the wound throbbed and stung. Blood seeped between my fingers, pumping out in time to my racing heart. Fear coiled in my stomach like an icy snake and then spread, turning my legs to jelly, and no matter how I screamed inside my head, I couldn't get my feet to move.

"Please," I whispered. "Please don't…"

"Who are you?" he demanded.

The world began to spin again, and my palm felt cold. My whole body too. "I don't understand what you—"

"He'll want her," the crouching man snapped like he was insisting on a point in an argument. "You need to hurry."

A snarl twisted the tall man's lip, and then his free hand rose fast, coming to his mouth.

He ripped his teeth through his own skin.

I gasped, but before I could do more than flinch back, he shifted his grip on my hair and shoved his wrist against my mouth.

Clamping my lips shut, I struggled against his hold, trying desperately to turn my face away. His fingers dug into my scalp; I could feel my hair ripping. But my body seemed too thick, like my muscles were turning to a tingling sort of clay. The world kept tipping and tilting, and a weird buzzing whine started in my head.

He yanked at my hair, jerking my head back hard, and a startled breath parted my lips.

Blood poured in, tasting like something rotten laced with metal, and it burned like fire. I choked, trying to spit it out, but he tugged my head back and shoved his wrist in harder, prying my jaw wide. Like molten metal, the blood filled my mouth and scorched my throat. I gagged, trying to scream, but I couldn't escape it. I couldn't even breathe.

Suddenly, I lurched upward only to topple down again as his grip vanished. I crashed onto something soft, and my stomach heaved as I choked, trying to get the viscous fire out of me. My head swam. I couldn't feel my legs or hands. Over the buzz-saw whine in my ears, I thought I heard shouting, but it was hard to focus on it. Everything was dark; my eyes weren't working right. And I was cold. So cold. Even the fiery blood couldn't help me, and as I tried to spit it out, sobs wracked my body. I wanted a blanket. Something warm. I just wanted to be warm and safe and for everything to stop hurting.

A dark shape moved in front of me, murky in the blur of moonlight. A guy's voice reached my ears: angry, swearing vehemently. The shadows grew thicker like they wanted to swallow him, and I couldn't make out his features in the dying shreds of moonlight.

"—hang on. Just hang on—"

Darkness swallowed him, and swallowed me too, dragging me away from the cold into a place where nothing hurt anymore.

**4**

---

ASHER

The rabids surrounded the dark-haired young woman, and even from a distance, I could smell her blood on the air.

Cursing blurred through my mind as I dove toward the bastards, Gideon and Ulysses at my side. From atop the cliff, two shadows took off like startled rabbits, fleeing into the night sky.

*Liam,* I sent along the connection between us.

He darted after them. I knew the bastards wouldn't get far.

Down in the cove, the other two rabids crowded in on the girl, trying to finish their feast. Gideon swept past me to hover above them, ready to catch them if they tried to follow their friends away from here.

The nearest rabid, a short man with clothes that probably belonged to one of his previous victims, spun when Ulysses and I hit land and shifted to human form. An aura of indefinable wrongness radiated from him like a corruption I could feel—the sensation enough to identify him as a rabid even if the bastard hadn't looked like death warmed over. His body reeked of staying too long outside civilization, where he'd probably fed on anything, alive or dead. Rabids didn't feed to gain the illusion of life. They didn't care about how our kind could breathe or how we possessed a heartbeat as long as we'd fed recently. They ate anything, purely for the fun of it.

And the more terror they wrought in their victim, the more fun they had.

Baring his rot-encrusted fangs in the moonlight, he lunged at Ulysses, tangling with him in a blur of shadow I knew the decaying bastard wouldn't survive. The one holding the young woman surged upward, attempting to take off with her in tow. Gideon snagged him and ripped him away from her, then took off after him when the bastard made a break for the river.

I caught the girl when she crumpled to the ground. She convulsed in my arms, her skin like ice. Blood covered her face, her neck, and stained her pale shirt, all of it smeared across her like a child had gone mad with finger paint.

And a ragged wound was torn in her throat.

I swore furiously, digging a bandage from one of the pockets of my pants and ignoring the sounds of Gideon dealing with the bastard who bit her. Goddamn *animals*. The wound was too big for me to heal, which meant she was bleeding out, and there wasn't a damn thing I could do about it except hope we could get her to a hospital in time. "Hang on," I urged the girl. "Just hang on."

"Asher!"

I looked up to see Gideon in human form, pinning the rabid twenty feet off the ground. The asshole snarled and snapped at him, not coming too close to the knife Gideon held at his throat. Keeping his one remaining eye on the bastard, my friend nodded to the rabid's arm.

A bite wound scored the rabid's wrist.

"*Shit.*" I looked back down at the young woman. There was so much blood, it was impossible to tell what was hers or his, but it didn't matter. The truth was clear.

They'd tried to turn her.

The girl's wide hazel eyes stared up at the night, and the gods only knew what she was seeing. A desperate, pleading expression contorted her face, and her mouth moved like she was trying to say something, but only frightened gurgles left her. And then even those became too much. Her body lurched, a look of such horrible pain in her eyes, and her gaze turned, locking on mine with frantic intensity, as if she was trying to hold herself to this life by willpower alone.

"Sentinel," she whispered.

Darkness thumped in my chest like a heartbeat not my own. The shadows spread fast, wrapping me and choking me with a touch whose horror hadn't faded even in memory. In a tingling wave, the black power encircled every cell of my body, gripping me as solidly as an anchor beneath the sea, tying me to a nightmare I thought I'd left behind centuries ago.

*Amalie.*

As suddenly as it had come, the sensation faded.

The girl's lids fluttered as her eyes rolled back. A

stilted breath shuddered from her, and then she sagged in my arms. Her chest became still.

I stared, frozen. This wasn't possible. It couldn't...

Gods below, please, no. We'd escaped. We'd been free. For the seven hundred *fucking* years since Amalie died, we'd—

Ulysses muttered a curse as he landed beside me, dusting his hands of any residual ash from the rabid. "Poor kid."

I jolted back, dropping the girl's limp body to the ground.

"Asher?" From the corner of my eye, I could see Ulysses staring at me. "What the hell, man?"

My mouth moved, wordless. But I couldn't say it. The others would panic if I did. Maybe even try to destroy themselves.

Before she could.

Overhead, shadows twisted as Liam continued to shred the other two rabids into nothing long after they'd probably already been annihilated. Several feet away, Ulysses waited for an answer I couldn't bring myself to give.

My eyes locked on the rabid whom Gideon still had pinned to the wall. At the jerk of my chin, he dragged the survivor down to the sand.

"Who is this?" I demanded.

A contemptuous look twisted the rabid's face, the expression made into a horror show by the girl's blood coating his chin.

"Asher," Ulysses said behind me. "What the hell is—"

"Don't touch her!" I snapped.

He held up his hands, backing away from the girl's body.

I returned my attention to the rabid. "Answer me and I'll make it quick. Who the *fuck* is this girl?"

The rabid chuckled. "Scared, Sentinel?"

My hands twitched to end him right now. "Why did you try to turn her? Your kind don't make friends with your food. Why try it with her?"

The man didn't respond.

I jerked my head at Gideon. Swiftly, he touched the blade of his knife to the rabid's throat. The man grunted, smoke rising from where the rune-engraved metal rested on his skin. Our weapons were far from ordinary steel. Forged half of the essence of angels, half of the blood of demons, the blades were keyed to us and us alone—an inexplicable gift we'd each woken to find in our grasp after we'd escaped death centuries ago. They existed somewhere between this reality and the world beyond, summoned from the ether whenever we needed them. When we wished, they glowed, and at other times they were dark metal that seemed to absorb all light, but they would always kill with scarcely any pressure on the blade.

And every rabid knew it.

"Why?" I repeated.

His face contorting with pain, he spat a curse at me. "Too late. You lonely soldiers, aimless for centuries. Eyeless." He scoffed at Gideon. "Voiceless." His eyes flicked up to where Liam still fought. "Too damaged inside to save anyone anymore." His gaze slid between me and Ulysses, and then his lips pulled back in a bloody grin, a mad sort of glee taking up residence in his gaze. "He's already won."

With a grunt, he shoved himself forward onto Gideon's knife, nearly decapitating himself on the blade.

"What in the—?" Gideon stepped back, his one good eye wide with alarm as the rabid began to turn to dust.

I didn't look away from the decaying body crumbling to the gravel.

"Zeus's balls," Ulysses snarled. "Does *anyone* care to explain what the fuck is going on?"

"Liam," I called rather than answer. "Enough already."

A moment passed, and then a sound like fabric in the wind came behind me as Liam landed, shifting seamlessly from shadow into his nearly colorless human form. Tatters of cloth and ash drifted down like dark snow around him, all that remained of the rabids.

"We must get the girl somewhere safe," Gideon said, tucking his knife away.

"Well, apparently we're not touching her," Ulysses retorted. "So that might be difficult."

"Why?" Liam rasped, his voice a harsh whisper.

Ulysses scoffed and jerked his chin at me. "Ask him."

Liam leaned into my line of sight, a questioning look on his pale face. *Asher?* he signed to me.

I turned back to the girl's corpse, unable to bring myself to respond. She was pretty—the blood all over her and the wound on her neck aside. Her hair looked nearly black in the darkness, the tousled waves lying as they'd fallen on the gravel and sand. She'd been young, too—late teens, maybe early twenties—with her whole life of sunlight ahead of her before the rabids brought that to an end.

I couldn't leave her here, though everything in me wanted to. Maybe the sunlight would take her. Maybe the protection we possessed wasn't hers to control any longer, and maybe her death now wouldn't kill us, any more than it had centuries ago.

*My noble Asher...*

I flinched away from the memory of her cold touch, of the blood on her hands. The girl in front of me looked nothing like the nightmare we'd escaped, but it didn't matter.

The bond was proof enough.

But if the sun didn't kill her, then leaving her here could prove a grave mistake. The rabids turned her. She'd be like them if we didn't get her the antidote in time, which meant I'd be risking leaving the humans to a slaughter when she woke.

Serial killers did less damage than a newly turned rabid left to their own devices.

But, moreover, the rabids wanted her. The gods knew why, considering they'd killed her seven hundred years before, but that didn't matter. Whatever they were after, it was a safe bet it wasn't good.

I strode toward the girl, bending fast to scoop her into my arms. A breath entered my lungs when nothing else happened, and without a word, I took off.

Flutters like fabric in the wind told me the others followed. They'd have questions, I was sure. But until she woke, I didn't know what to tell them. Maybe I was wrong. Maybe I'd just imagined it.

But if I wasn't, we were doomed.

Because the bloody queen of the vampires had returned.

5

WREN

There was only darkness and the fire, and in it, I burned. My skin howled beneath the onslaught; my bones turned to ash. But I couldn't stop it. Couldn't escape it.

Couldn't die.

I screamed in the night, surrounded by endless nothing, infinity swallowing my desperate cries. And no one heard me. No one came for me.

Saved me.

In the eternal void, I turned to ash and darkness too. All light, all warmth vanished, becoming a fantasy I'd foolishly believed in, once upon a time.

And then even that was gone.

Cold, alone, with nothing left of me but blackened dust, I floated in the darkness. I could slip away. Already, my mind was going, memories drifting off like tiny embers to be extinguished by the weight of the never-ending night. Home faded. Family. Friends too.

And pain.

Nothing hurt anymore. Nothing ever would. I was safe. Free. I could just… go.

And then, in the darkness, there came a whisper, cold and dripping with the malice of gods who grin while they watch the stars die.

*Not yet.*

<hr>

My eyelids were heavy. I could barely open them.

"There you are, sweet," came a woman's voice. "Careful. Take your time."

My brow furrowed. I couldn't see very well. Everything was dim, as if somebody had turned almost all the lights off. Something soft was beneath me. A bed, maybe, with pillows propping up my head. But the person speaking had an accent, sort of French but not quite, and she definitely didn't sound like my mom.

Was I in the hospital?

Memory flashed through me in a burst of fiery adrenaline. The man. The cove by the river. He'd tried—

"It's okay." Gentle fingers brushed my forehead in a soothing gesture. "You're safe, I promise."

My mouth moved, but all that came out was a wordless croak. I tried to look toward where I could hear the woman's voice, finding only a blurry form in what looked like a white lab coat. A doctor? But where were my parents? Why—

Dull throbbing stopped my thoughts in their tracks, as if my body just realized I'd woken up. In fits and starts, pain radiated from my stomach, spreading to my chest, my limbs, my head. My mouth clamped shut, but whimpers still escaped me. I twisted blindly, trying to escape the aching.

"Shh, I know, I know." A hand slipped beneath me, pulling me up. "Here."

Something that felt like a cup nudged at my mouth, and then warm liquid slipped between my lips. My throat convulsed in spite of myself, swallowing.

The pain dimmed instantly like the world's best aspirin had just gone to work. Blindly, I reached up, taking the cup around the woman's hand.

"That's right."

I drained the contents and didn't resist when she lowered me back to the soft bed again. Shudders still quivered through me like aftershocks of an earthquake, but the pain was leaving. Squeezing my eyes shut and then opening them again, I tried to get my vision to focus.

"Where—" I rasped.

A pause followed. "North City Clinic."

I didn't recognize the name. My eyes were starting to work better, though. There *was* a doctor standing next to me, a tall woman with dark skin and short hair. The name Sissoko was embroidered in blue lettering above the breast of her long white lab coat, while a blouse the color of emeralds showed beneath it.

"Wh-what happened?" I asked. "Are my mom and dad—"

A flicker of pity moved over the woman's face, and the small expression drove a spike of fear straight through me.

"Can you tell me your name, sweet?" she asked gently. "Do you remember?"

I blinked at her. "M-my name? Why..."

Her expression took on an edge of insistence, and I couldn't understand the reason. Why in the world would she think I couldn't remember my own name?

"Wren," I said. "Wren Cortwright."

A small smile crossed the woman's face. "It's nice to meet you, Wren. I'm Doctor Mariam Sissoko."

"Hi." I looked around the room. My eyes were clearing, and I blinked, freezing in place when I realized a man sat in the corner, nearly lost in the shadows. He wore gear that seemed like it belonged to a special ops soldier: a vest, a belt with weapons, a black shirt with equally black cargo pants and steel-toed boots. His dark hair was cropped short, and his face was formed of all sharp angles and planes, like a sculptor had carved him on a particularly angry day.

But the effect was stunning. Savage but cultured, a blade in human form. With eyes that could have been any color in the shadows, he watched me, unblinking, his elbows propped on his knees and his hands folded. Utterly blank patience emanated from him, as if he fully intended to sit there until the sun exploded—or until I became a threat.

A strange feeling tangled in me when I looked at him, hot and blurry, rushing through my body and making the room feel not quite real anymore. As if here and *somewhere else* merged, transforming the sight of the man before me.

*His hands on my skin. His mouth pressed to mine.*

*Thrusting harder and harder, he drove his cock into me as I arched beneath him, pleasure rolling through my naked body and—*

"Don't worry about him," Doctor Sissoko said to me.

I flinched back against the pillows, my cheeks burning. Whoa. What the *hell*...

Clearing my throat, I pulled my attention back to the doctor, not quite sure how I was supposed to ignore the terrifying soldier watching me like he was waiting for me to make one wrong move—let alone the fact my mind turned into a fully immersive porno when I looked at him. "Am...Am I under arrest or something?" I managed.

Doctor Sissoko chuckled. "No, not at all."

"Where are my parents?"

Pity flashed across her face again. "Your parents aren't going to be able to come, Wren."

Fear shot through me like a sudden rush of ice. "Why not? Are they okay? That man, did he—"

"It's not like that."

I stared at her, horrified, waiting. There was something so terribly implacable about her voice, that I couldn't even—

Breathe.

My hand flew to my mouth. My nose. I wasn't breathing. Oh my God, why wasn't I breathing?

"Wren," the doctor began. "Something happened when that man—"

"Where are my parents?" I shoved at the mattress, but my body still felt weak. When I tried to move for the side of the bed, my legs didn't want to respond. "I want to see my mom and dad. I—"

Doctor Sissoko's hands pressed on my shoulders, stopping me. "I need you to listen to me, sweet."

I pushed at her, panic strengthening me, and the doctor stumbled back. The guy in the chair was on his feet instantly, like an attack dog on alert, a long silver knife somehow in his fist even if I hadn't seen him draw the blade. The metal glinted strangely in the dim light, somehow brighter than it should have been.

Doctor Sissoko made a quick calming gesture. "It's okay. Please."

I couldn't tell if she was talking to him or me, but I didn't care. While the guy tucked the knife away somewhere I couldn't see, I clambered out of the bed, staggering when my bare feet hit the linoleum floor. I was wearing a hospital gown, white with little blue flowers on it, and I couldn't see my clothes anywhere. "I want out of here. Now. You can't keep me."

"The man who attacked you," Doctor Sissoko said as if I hadn't even spoken. "He bit you. Do you remember?"

I stared at her, my hand lifting to my neck and finding a thick bandage there. Of course I remembered. It'd been insane. It—

His teeth. The squat guy, when he grinned at me, his teeth had been spiked like fangs. And then the other man bit his wrist and—

I flinched away from the memory. "I want to go home."

"After he bit you," the doctor continued like I hadn't spoken, "you died, Wren. You've been dead for three nights."

Trembling spread inside me until the ground didn't feel stable anymore. My eyes darted from her to the soldier, blinking, and my mouth moved. I couldn't make a sound.

A patient look took up residence on Doctor Sissoko's face. "Some people, when they're bitten like that, they don't wake up. You did. But that still means things have changed for you."

"No." I shook my head, more certain by the second. "No, where is he? Is this some kind of—"

"He's dead. But this isn't a joke or a trick. I promise you."

"Bullshit."

She paused like she was trying to decide how to proceed. "What I just gave you wasn't medicine, Wren. It was blood. Because when that man bit you and then made you drink his—"

I choked on a shriek and ran for the door.

The soldier guy reached it before I made it two steps.

I slammed to a halt, staring at him while the room seemed to waver around me. He was nothing but lean muscle, and somehow I knew if I took off that black shirt, he'd be like marble, but scarred on his shoulders and back. A circular scar from a burn here, a long line from a whip there. He wasn't bulky like some performer in the World Wrestling Federation, but he was strong as hell in body and mind alike...and the gods knew I'd enjoyed every second of breaking that.

I trembled. Breaking... what? Him? Why the hell was I even *thinking* about...

He took a step closer to me, and it was everything I could do not to whimper. Every line of his body spoke of strength and skill, like someone trained at killing and damn well good at it, while his clothes made him look like a contender for Hot Soldier of the Year. His face gave him the look of being in his twenties, but his eyes...

Darker blue than a lapis lazuli, nearly gunmetal gray. They were beautiful—and wrong. All wrong. No twenty-something-year-old had eyes like that. Eyes that looked like they'd seen more than somebody who lived to be a hundred. Eyes that wanted to pry me apart, if only to reveal every last one of my secrets.

"It's okay, Asher," the doctor said.

He ignored her completely. "Who are you?" he asked me, his voice low and careful, like a knife at the edge of breaking skin. "Really?"

A tremor went through me, pulling me apart, as if my body wanted to move toward him while my instincts wanted to flee. I chose door number two, stepping back and trying to keep him and the doctor in view at the same time.

Doctor Sissoko glanced at him briefly and then returned her attention to me. "The man who attacked you was what we call a rabid. Normally, when bitten by a rabid, you would become one as well, but Asher and others were able to bring you here for the antidote in time. However, that only spares you from becoming as he is. It still means you are like us." She paused. "A vampire."

I shook my head, an incredulous scoff bubbling up inside me. "No. That isn't...Why are you..."

She sighed. "Because I've been doing this for a very long time, and I've learned it's usually best to simply tell people the truth."

I shook my head again, as if, of every motion in the

universe, it was the only one that could cover this. Because none of what she said could be true. None of it. "Y-you're lying. You... you just sighed. You're breathing. This is a trick. You—"

"As will you, once your body has time to adjust. When you feed, your body can emulate life as humans know it. Breathing, heartbeat, all of that will come back to you. But you're still very new to this. You can't push yourself too hard, so you should take it slow at the start." The doctor motioned to the bed. "There's a great deal I need to explain, Wren. Would you come sit down?"

I sputtered. Like hell I'd sit there and listen to this... this *madness.* "I-I'm talking. How could I be talking if I'm not breathing? No, you... you've done something to me. This isn't—"

"The same forces that keep you in this life enable certain conveniences. It will make sense if you allow me to explain."

My head shook. Make *sense*? How the hell—

Asher took a step toward me. "Did you know the man who attacked you?"

A rough noise left me, somewhere between a scoff and a shriek. This couldn't be real. I was dreaming.

I bumped into the wall and realized I'd backed up into it.

"Had you ever seen him before?" he continued.

His dark eyes searched mine, and I looked away, unable to withstand the scrutiny. I couldn't hope to respond to him. I couldn't even think because this? This wasn't *happening.*

"Wren," Doctor Sissoko started.

"Shut up." I shrank from her words, my body drawing down into a crouch by the wall.

"Asher and his team simply need to know if—"

"I said *shut up!*" I crumbled further into a ball, wrapping my arms around my head like maybe it'd stop her words. "You're lying. You're all lying."

For a long moment, the doctor was silent and the guy was too.

"We'll give you some time," Doctor Sissoko said quietly.

I trembled, feeling like at any moment I was going to fly apart. Scatter into atoms and drown in this chaos.

The door closed. I wrapped my arms tighter around myself and sobbed, only to freeze with horror when I realized I couldn't even feel tears in my own eyes.

And then all I could do was scream.

**6**

———

ULYSSES

The door shut behind Asher, and a moment later, the girl began to scream.

"Holy shit," I sputtered, shoving away from where I'd leaned on the wall. "What did you do to her?"

Doc Sissoko motioned reassuringly. "It's fine, Ulysses. Honestly, she's doing rather well."

I stared at the woman. Seriously? The sound was horrible. Agonized. The kind of noise somebody made when they were trapped inside a fiery building, burning alive. And yeah, okay, so it'd been a long time since the four of us had done more than drop off victims at the clinic—which explained jack shit about why we were still here after three whole nights—so maybe this was common.

But *sounds of immolation* didn't exactly fit my definition of "doing well."

"You sure somebody shouldn't, you know, be in there

to help her?" I eyed the door, not sure what I'd do but damn well ready to try *something*. Doc Sissoko may have been tending to the newly turned for the better part of two centuries ever since a rabid bit her back in Mali, and she'd done more for revolutionizing methods of care in that time than anyone else in the past thousand years, but god of the underworld, how could she not be panicking to hear that horrible sound?

"I promise." Doc smiled. "Some people react this way. The shock just... They have to express it somehow. But we have cameras in the room, and my people are monitoring her. If she seems like she's in danger, we'll go back in to help her. Until then, we're simply giving her space to process this in her own time. She'll be all right."

Nodding slowly and trying to believe her, I glanced at Asher, who as yet hadn't said a word. Not that that was unusual; the guy was normally tight-lipped about every-thing. But after nearly a millennium, I also knew the man.

Something was still bugging him and given the fact he'd been weird as hell about us even touching the girl, it wasn't a huge leap to assume that *something* was her.

"Okay," I allowed. "So then, what gives? What's the deal with the new girl?"

The doc looked back and forth between us. "I'm not sure I understand your question."

"Was there something odd about the rabids who attacked her? Did she remember anything unusual?"

Doc Sissoko shook her head. "Not that she's said thus far. Though I have to warn you, she may not recall. Some-times victims don't remember much of the assault. Their minds shut down in an attempt to protect them from the trauma."

"Gotcha." I didn't take my eyes from Asher, who was watching the closed door like he could see straight through it to the girl. And it didn't make sense. Yeah, she was hot. Like hellfire, really—the fact she'd been covered in blood when I first saw her aside. But that didn't do much to explain why Mister Responsibility here was hung up on her. I was pretty sure the last time Asher so much as slept with a woman, vampire or otherwise, corsets had been standard issue and humans were painting their skin with lead.

"So, I guess that's it then, right?" I prompted him. "Doc's got her. She's going to be fine. We should probably get on tracking down the rest of that rabid nest, yeah?" A moment passed. "Asher?"

He turned back toward me, blinking as if trying to refocus. "What?"

Every instinct I possessed started clamoring in alarm. I glanced from him to the doc and back. "Uh, okay, man. Can I talk to you for a sec?" I nodded my head down the hall and then started that way.

Asher followed me a short distance from the doc.

"What gives?" I tried. "You've been acting weird ever since we found the girl."

"Wren."

"Huh?"

Asher looked back at me. "Her name. Wren."

I hesitated. Nice name. Also, not the point. "Okay, *Wren*. But that doesn't answer my question. What's—"

The thunderous pulse of an explosion cut me off. The

floor shuddered hard, making us stumble, and the overhead panels cut out for a second, only to be replaced by emergency lighting. Dust rained from the ceiling.

Screams rose from farther in the building, in the direction of the main entrance.

Doc Sissoko made an anxious noise, but Asher moved fast, catching her when she took a step toward the sound.

"My staff," the doc protested. "If there's been an accident—"

"We'll check it out," Asher said.

"But we have oxygen tanks for non-vampire patients," she argued. "If one of them exploded, then people may need my help."

The faint sounds of distant growls reached my ears. Asher met my eyes, the same *oh fuck* look on his face as I knew had to be on mine.

"Guard the doctor," he snapped at me and then took off running toward the sound.

Doc Sissoko looked between us, clearly torn on whether she wanted to be guarded at all. "My people—"

"We'll take care of them." I moved her as firmly as I could toward the girl's room. "Get in there with Wren."

"Ulysses—"

"This isn't an accident. I need you to get back in—"

Nurses raced past the turn of the hallway to my left, running as if for their lives. On their heels, a pair of rabids tore around the corner, leaping at them from behind.

The nurses fell. With claws and teeth, the rabids tore into them as they screamed.

Doc Sissoko cried out in horror, her hand flying to her mouth. She started toward the nurses as if to help, and I snagged her arm, stopping her. There wasn't anything we could do for them. Already, their blood was everywhere on the floor and walls. In a few moments more, their bodies would turn to dust.

But at the doc's cry, the rabids' heads snapped toward us. A man and a woman, their hair matted and their clothes looking nearly rotted from their bodies, like they'd crawled straight from a grave to come here. The sense of *wrong* that marked a rabid, at least to my kind, radiated from them like an oil slick on the air. Blood dripping down their faces, they grinned.

I swore, shoving the doc behind me as the pair scrambled off their victims and charged toward us. In an instant, my knife was in my grip, called from the ether and materializing at my command. I ran at them, dropping to my knees to slide across the tile as the nearest rabid leapt at me. I slashed at her as I passed, my blade slicing through her neck and taking her head. The other came straight at me, and I shoved back up from the ground, colliding with the rabid and then using his momentum to whip myself around him and drive the weapon into his spine.

The man disintegrated. The woman was already gone.

I threw a quick look back at the hall they'd come from. More cries rang out from farther in the building. Asher and the others would be there, hopefully. But until we had the building secured, this wasn't over by far.

And there was no way in hell I could let them kill the doc or the girl.

Keeping my knife in hand, I strode back toward Doc Sissoko. "You need to hide. Get in that room and barricade the door. You understand me?"

She shook her head, looking dazed. "My staff—"

"We'll help them. But we need you safe. Please."

Her mouth moved in silent protest, but she followed as I pulled her toward the room. As I reached the door, I paused. "You know where all the cameras in the room are?"

She nodded.

"Disconnect them. Block them. Whatever you can do. If these guys reach the monitors, I don't want them spotting you in there, understand?"

Swallowing hard, she nodded again.

Hugging her knees in a corner, Wren stared when I opened the door. "Who's this?" she stammered, looking terrified at the sight of me. "What's going on?"

Holy hell, she really was beautiful. Hair like polished wood, skin like porcelain. Eyes like a boulder opal, lost between green and blue and brown. Gods, you could fall into those and not even mind if you drowned.

*Stay focused, idiot.*

I tried for my best smile. "Hey there, I'm Ulysses. Don't worry. Everything'll be fine." The words were a bald-faced lie, but I didn't know how to answer her, considering the truth would only make her more scared. "Lock this," I said to the doc. "Put something in front of it, if you can. But don't open it up until you hear from us."

Doc Sissoko nodded. Her face tense, she closed the door behind me, sealing herself and Wren inside.

Adjusting my grip on my knife, I looked either way down the hall. The screams seemed to be coming from throughout the sprawling medical complex now. The cries sounded closer, too, though I hadn't seen any more rabids accompanying them.

I checked the handle to make sure it was locked and then planted myself in front of the door, ready for the first rabid who made the mistake of coming down this hall.

**7**

---

WREN

I stared at the doctor as she dragged the bed over to block the door. "What's happening?"

Doctor Sissoko turned, scanning the ceiling. "It's going to be okay."

Nervousness prickled through me. That's not what someone said when things were fine. That's what they said when you were screwed. And then there was Ulysses, another contender for Hot Soldier of the Year who'd just disappeared out the door. He was as tall as Asher, lean and dark-haired too, but with a warmth Asher hadn't possessed and a smile that set my heart fluttering in spite of everything.

And, God Almighty, the things that had flashed through my mind when I saw him. Sex hot enough to set the bed on fire. Things he could do with his mouth and tongue that would make me die of ecstasy. Somehow, even if I swore I'd never seen him before in my life, I knew his body was nothing but solid muscle below that cocksure grin.

I also seriously doubted he locked people in rooms at random.

Moving quickly, the doctor grabbed a chair, dragging it toward the corner to the left of the door. Emergency lighting shone from a pair of spotlights on the wall, casting her in eerie brightness and shadow. Climbing onto the chair, she reached up and grabbed a tiny black device I hadn't noticed perched in the corner.

Wait, was that a *camera*? "What—"

Something crashed farther in the building, making the floor quiver.

Doctor Sissoko threw a glance at the door. Hopping down from the chair, she hefted it under one arm and carried it with her to the corner next to me. Positioning it quickly, she climbed up again and yanked down another small device near the ceiling.

I stared at her. This was a trick too. It had to be. Somewhere in the past few minutes, before the lights cut out and this latest madness began, my heart had started pounding and my breaths came fast. And I'd realized the truth.

These people had to be lying to me.

I wasn't a *vampire*. That was psychotic. These people had drugged me, plain and simple. I only *thought* I hadn't been breathing before, maybe through some trick of hypnosis—which they *clearly* knew would wear off, so they told me this vampire story. And yeah, I didn't know why those men with weird teeth attacked me, or why these people had me here, but I wasn't what they claimed.

I was fine, and at my first opportunity, I was getting the hell out of here and going home.

A thud came from the door, and all my thoughts cut off. The doctor froze. Both of us stared at the entrance.

Snarls came from the other side, and then shrieks too as the sound of fighting suddenly broke out beyond the solid surface. Something crashed into the wall, sending a framed picture toppling to the ground, and more snarls followed, like a dogfight tumbling away from the door.

Shivers gripped me. In the stark emergency lighting, I suddenly felt entirely too visible.

Doctor Sissoko glanced at me, putting a finger to her lips. I couldn't even nod in response.

Another thud came on the door, harder.

Her face lined with tension, the doctor glanced around the room as if checking for something, and then shook her head, frustration flickering through her expression. Climbing back onto the chair, she reached up and carefully pushed the tile of the drop ceiling aside from its crosshatch of supports. Hissing softly for my attention, she motioned for me to stand.

Another thud. The frame around the door cracked.

I scrambled to my feet as the doctor got down from the chair.

"Go on." She jerked her chin toward the opening. "There should be beams you can use for support. I'll be right behind you."

I threw a nervous look between the ceiling and the door and then got on the chair. Fumbling in the dark above the tiles, my hands found a dusty metal strut.

"Good," the doctor whispered. "Now just jump..."

I did as she said. She caught my legs and hefted me upward with more strength than it seemed like her thin frame should possess. Clambering onto the support, I tugged my legs through the opening and then worked my way around on my stomach until I was facing the hole. "Come on," I whispered, reaching down for her.

Another thud came from the door.

The doctor gave me a tense smile and then vanished into dark smoke.

I froze.

The cloud rose through the opening in the ceiling and then reformed into the doctor crouched on the beam across from me. She smiled at me again, friendly this time and encouraging too, and then pushed the ceiling tile back into place.

Maybe it wasn't hypnosis. Maybe I was just dreaming.

"Go on, Wren," the woman whispered.

Swallowing against my mouth gone totally dry, I hesitated. Did I want my back to whatever she was?

Did I have a choice?

And if it was a dream, it didn't matter, right? I'd be fine. This was just—

"Wren?" she pressed.

Trembling, I shimmied around on the beam and then crept forward. The darkness was eerie. Not complete even though surely it should have been, considering there were no lights up here. But I could still see so much in it. The metal supports were cast in a weird silver shimmer that suggested colors without ever quite becoming them. The wires and pipes all around me were the same, glinting with a bizarre sheen of not-quite-color, and when I glanced back, the doctor was too.

The emergency lights. That had to be it. They must be getting past the ceiling tiles somehow.

"Go that way." Doctor Sissoko twitched her chin forward. "I'll be right behind you."

I started crawling. Grit and dust caked the beam beneath me, and I gripped the metal as hard as I could. It was only a few inches wide. At any moment, I felt like I'd lose my balance and—

A crash came from behind and below me. I froze, clutching the beam and trying not to topple sideways while I threw a desperate look over my shoulder.

The doctor was gone. Snarls rose from the vicinity of the room I'd just left.

Clamping my lips shut on a whimper, I kept crawling. Surely, the doctor had a plan. Maybe she'd turned back into a shadow-thing, and that's why I couldn't see her, though that was hardly comforting. It was barely even sane, considering it should have been impossible. But this was just a dream, really, so *surely*, she—

The tiles beside me erupted upward, and a man surged through the gap. His teeth were fangs, and the reek of rotted meat surrounded him like a cloud. Stains covered his clothes, and his hands were filthy. At the sight of him, a weird sensation hit me like a bell inside my head clanging *wrong, wrong, wrong.* He grabbed my leg, hauling on me, and I screamed, clutching the beam with all my might.

A dark shadow buffeted me like a sudden wind and struck the man, knocking him back down through the hole in the ceiling. Doctor Sissoko reappeared below, gripping his arms and fighting to keep him from coming after me.

"Go, Wren!" she shouted.

I stared, horrified. I couldn't just leave her.

*Kill him.*

My body spasmed with the sudden, irrational urge to lunge down there and tear into the man with my bare hands. I clutched the metal strut harder, fighting the lunatic impulse.

The man tried to twist in Doctor Sissoko's grasp. She caught his arm, wrenching it back behind him and making him cry out in pain. Instantly, he turned to smoke, only for her to do the same and collide with him. They both reappeared, the doctor still gripping the man's arms to hold him in place.

"Go!" Doctor Sissoko grunted with effort as the man tried to break free. "Wren, go now!"

Shame and fear crushing me, I made myself start crawling. Snarls and crashes rose from behind me, the sounds of the fight I'd left the poor doctor to face alone. But then what could I have done? I'd never been in a fight in my life. And maybe it was a trick. More things to convince me... *something*, though I didn't have a clue what. But I couldn't hear her shouting. Maybe everything was fine.

Maybe she was dead.

I crawled faster. I couldn't tell anything from the sounds behind me, which meant she could be okay. Perhaps the threat *wasn't* a trick, but she could stop him, and then she'd come back up here and—

The beam reached its end at a dark, cinderblock wall. Throwing a desperate look over my shoulder, I checked for Doctor Sissoko, but she wasn't there. Crashing sounds still came from the room, fainter now over the distance, but that was it. And nothing came from beneath me.

There wasn't anywhere else to go.

Swallowing hard, I reached down and levered up one of the tiles with my fingernails. The room beneath me was an eerie replica of the one I'd just left, minus the monster lunging up through the opening to attack. I hesitated, waiting for anything to appear in the hole, and then wriggled around until I could drop my legs through the gap. My hands ached as I lowered myself down, and when I dropped to the floor, I bit back a grunt when my ankle twinged.

The room was empty save for the hospital bed and a plastic chair in the corner. I glanced at the hole in the ceiling and then headed for the door. For a moment, I listened, but none of the sounds of fighting seemed to be coming closer.

God, I needed to get out of here.

I eased the door open and peeked outside only to freeze, a tiny, choked noise escaping me. At the end of the long hall to my right, dark liquid splattered the walls like someone had tried to recreate a Jackson Pollock painting. A sharp and metallic tang carried on the air, and my brain filled in the blank with the certain knowledge it was blood. I couldn't see any bodies, though. Only swaths of dust like a chimney sweep had thrown a fit.

But that soldier guy, Ulysses, wasn't there. The doctor either. Swallowing hard to keep my stomach down, I checked the hall straight ahead of me and then crept from the doorway.

Another crash came from the room far down the hall. The door exploded outward, a body tumbling with it in a shower of woodchips.

The man staggered to his feet, snarling. His body was a mess of bruised skin and bloodied gashes, and he stumbled as if barely able to stay upright. In the stark emergency lighting, he looked like a cross between a zombie and a homicidal maniac, and the same clanging bell of wrong went off in my head at the sight of him. He lurched back toward the room and then paused, whipping his head to the side as he spotted me.

I took off running.

A snarl like a wild animal came from the man. I knew he'd be chasing me, like a rabbit knows the wolf is on its heels. I bolted down the corridor, my bare feet hitting hard on the linoleum and my hospital gown feeling like nothing between me and the monster. The white doors to my right were closed, and I didn't have much hope they'd keep him out, anyway. To my left, there was only a wall made of cinderblocks painted mint green. The corridor branched ahead, and I tore down the hall to the left, hoping the blank wall on that side meant it faced the exterior.

And that sooner or later, there'd be a door.

A pained shout came from behind me, and I risked a frantic glance over my shoulder. Ulysses was there, attacking the man chasing me. He slashed at the guy with a long knife while the man ducked back, avoiding the strike. Another two guys in ragged clothes were tearing down the hall, though, aiming for me or the soldier attacking their friend, I didn't know.

*Kill them all.*

My body lurched like a marionette tugged two different directions by its strings, and I staggered, my limbs suddenly not cooperating with my desire to run. Panic gripped me as I caught the wall to keep from falling. What the hell was *wrong* with me?

Shivers ran over my skin. Nothing, that's what. I was fine.

The two guys leapt past Ulysses, flying through the air like they were Olympic runners and he was a hurdle. Sheer adrenaline overrode everything else in my head, and I whirled, bolting down the corridor. Another turn lay ahead, and when I rounded the corner, the red glow of an exit sign waited above a fire door at the end of the hall.

Relief rushed through me like cold water, lending me an extra burst of speed. I raced toward the exit and slammed into the crossbar handle, shoving it aside.

A cement stairwell waited on the other side, winding upward through beams of white emergency lighting and thick shadow. All around it, there were no other doors. Nothing but the hall behind me and a stairway ahead. A frantic shriek of frustration left me, and then I scrambled upward. My hand clutched the metal rail, hauling me up the steps faster. My bare feet scraped on the rough cement. I couldn't hear anyone behind me, but that didn't mean somebody wouldn't be coming. I didn't dare slow down.

The stairs felt endless, climbing into infinity, and doubt gnawed at me like a dog with a bone. Maybe I was going the wrong way. Maybe this would take me to a rooftop, and I'd truly be trapped. Why in the world would they have these endless stairs going *up* in this—

I rounded a turn and nearly whimpered with relief at the sight of a door atop the next flight. Racing up the steps, I grabbed for the handle.

It turned, but the door wouldn't budge.

A panicked cry escaped me, and I yanked on the lever again and again. The lock held, trapping me inside.

The sound of fighting came from farther down the stairwell.

Terror shot through me, making every nerve in my body go on alert for any monsters racing up the stairs. I flung myself at the door, slamming into it with my shoulder.

The lock shattered and the door flew wide. I staggered out, shaking all over, and for a moment, all I could do was gape at the dent in the shape of my shoulder marring the metal. That wasn't normal. I couldn't—

Must've been a cheap door.

Clinging to the thought, I spun, surveying wherever I'd ended up. It looked like a massive shed, the kind park rangers used to store their equipment. An ambulance and two white vans were parked behind enormous garage doors, while suits like firefighters would wear hung from hooks on the left wall.

What the hell was this place?

I spotted a person-sized exit in the corner beyond the ambulances, and I took off running. Unlike the door in the stairwell, the lock to this one gave way much easier, breaking after only one sharp tug.

Which meant nothing. They really should have gotten better locks.

Trees surrounded me when I raced outside, and only a narrow road led from the building into the woods. Everything not touched by the glow of the security lamps glimmered with that strange cast of silver I'd seen when crawling along the ceiling beams in the complex below.

Which, of course, was just a trick of the light.

I raked a hand through my hair before realizing how utterly filthy I probably was. I was barefoot in a hospital gown in what looked like the middle of nowhere. I had to get away from here, and I didn't have any other option. It wasn't like I could hot-wire an ambulance.

And those people would be coming.

I ran for the forest.

**8**

---

ASHER

My knife tore through the rabid lunging at my throat, and with a scream, the man disintegrated.

Brushing the dust from myself, I muttered a curse and threw a quick look toward Liam. I'd found him fighting a trio of the bastards down near the lobby, and we'd been working together to clear the halls of them ever since. Through the connection between us all, I could tell Ulysses and Gideon were doing the same elsewhere in the complex.

But gods, there were a lot of these things.

The rabid in front of Liam took one look at both of us and then threw herself at his blade.

With a rasp of frustration, Liam yanked his knife away, but it was too late. The rabid grinned even as she crumbled into dust before him.

He turned to me, signing fast. *What is going* on *with these creatures?*

I shook my head. All of them were the same. The rabids attacked, killed as many as they could, and then suicided if it looked like they might be caught. Even deliberately trying to save them hadn't been enough. They ripped out their own throat if they couldn't get access to our weapons.

I'd started to wonder if every rabid in the world had gone insane.

*Crazy bastards.* Liam signed, surveying the wreckage that was the surgical wing. The attackers had come down one of the elevators and blown up the shaft in their wake. It was anyone's guess how they found us in the first place, but hopefully some staff had made it out through the clinic's alternate exits.

The gods knew too many others hadn't escaped.

I let my knife dematerialize. "Can you get back to the surface? Check on the condition up there?"

Liam nodded.

He headed for the hall that led to one of the emergency stairwells that dotted the sprawling clinic. One led to the house above, others to the woods surrounding the old farmhouse that was the topside face of the underground clinic. Still more exits lay on the fringes of the property, in storage sheds or garages. The clinic housed everything from emergency surgery to a psych ward, all sprawled across three levels and below approximately two square miles of forest and farmland.

Brushing dust from my arms, I turned and jogged back through the halls toward the administrative offices. I'd gotten more of a glimpse of the layout of the clinic in my mad dash to catch the rabids than I'd had in the past hundred years. Once upon a time, these corridors had been a rat's nest of mines. Now, they held the largest vampire medical facility in the state.

And every rabid had been willing to die rather than tell us why they attacked it.

"Goddammit!" Gideon shouted from somewhere up ahead. I picked up speed, summoning my knife back into my fist as I ran. Coming around the turn, I spotted him fending off a rabid who had him backed into a corner.

And gods below, the bastard was big. Easily almost seven feet tall, with arms so huge, they looked like bowling balls had been used in place of his muscles. Scars covered his face, as if someone had gone at him with a cheese grater. His clothes were in better shape than most rabids—fewer stains, fewer holes. He probably hadn't been turned too long ago.

It only made him more dangerous.

I raced at him, crossing the distance past the nurses' station in only a moment. Leaping at the guy, I snagged the rabid's arm with my own and used my momentum to throw him off-balance. As I hit the ground, I hooked his ankle and shifted my weight fast, sending him toppling to the tile floor. Releasing my knife back into the ether, I snatched a manacle from my equipment belt and slammed the metal around the rabid's wrist.

"Son of a—" Gideon snarled.

"Grab that arm!" I ordered, struggling to hold the rabid down. The man was attempting to push me off like I was a child playing at wrestling with him.

Gideon grabbed at the man's wrist, succeeding in pinning it on the third try.

"What in the gods—" Ulysses' voice came from behind us.

I threw a look over my shoulder to find him by one of the corridors, Doctor Sissoko at his back. "What are you doing here?" I demanded of him.

"Girl ran. I'm trying to find her."

The rabid howled, cutting off my reply. Snarling, the man thrashed as if intending to do us the favor of ripping him apart. With the enchanted metal wrapping his wrist, he couldn't shift into shadows, but that didn't stop him from struggling.

Cursing, I fought to hang on to the guy. "Take his arm. No weapons!"

Ulysses appeared beside me. "I'm guessing you don't mean take it off."

"Dammit, Ulysses. Grab his fucking arm!"

The man pinned the rabid down, avoiding the guy's attempt to throw himself toward a blade. "Not this time, asshole," Ulysses snarled.

"They've been killing themselves where you were, too?" Gideon grunted, fighting to keep the rabid restrained.

"Just like the one at the river."

My attention on the rabid, I stepped back. His struggles weren't stopping. If anything, he seemed to be becoming more frantic.

I summoned my knife.

The man's eyes locked on me, and his thrashing slowed. A cold twitch pulled at his lip, a hint of satisfaction amid the hate in his expression.

"You want us to kill you," I said.

Contempt twisted his face, but eagerness was there too. "You don't have the balls. I know what you are. Sentinel. *Failure*. Couldn't even save your queen or all the city that burned when she—"

Ulysses' elbow slammed into the man's jaw, knocking his head sideways. The rabid growled as he turned back to us again.

I regarded him coldly. "Goading us won't work."

Frustration flashed across the man's face.

"Why did you attack this place?" I continued.

He scoffed at me.

"Why are you willing to die rather than speak to us?"

"Think yourselves so special, don't you?" he retorted.

"Ah, so it's not about us, then?"

The man glared.

Right.

I looked around the hall while Gideon and Ulysses continued to hold the man down. There was only one unifying factor between here and the river, and she'd apparently managed to make a run for it right when rabids decided to attack this place.

Convenient.

And yet more proof I wasn't dealing with someone who was the innocent victim she appeared to be.

My skin crawled when I looked back at the man. "Who's the girl?"

For less than a heartbeat, fear flashed behind his eyes.

"What's so special about her?" Besides being the source of all my nightmares. "Why does she matter to you?"

"What girl?" the man sneered.

Ulysses scoffed. "Oh, you'll never make it in Hollywood."

"You came here for her," I said, ignoring him. "Tell me why, and we'll make it quick."

The man glared at me, seething.

"Come on, you great bloody mammoth," Gideon snarled. "You want us to take our time getting answers out of you?"

The rabid's eyes slid from Ulysses to Gideon, contempt in his expression, before he looked back up at me. "I'll be waiting for you in hell, Sentinel." Closing his eyes, he began chanting, the words like twisted versions of the ancient language of the vampires, though I hadn't heard them in centuries.

His skin reddened as if suddenly becoming sunburnt. Around Ulysses and Gideon's grip, his flesh started bubbling. Cracking. Blackening around the edges of each open sore. Steam and wisps of smoke rose from the man.

Ulysses recoiled. "What the—"

"Get back!" Gideon shouted, grabbing Ulysses and retreating quickly.

The rabid screamed as his body burst into flames.

I backed away fast, staring as the man's body was consumed by fire. He thrashed in the blaze, the motions seeming involuntary because he made no move to try to save himself. The smoke hit the detectors overhead, and a cascade of water sprayed down from the sprinklers in the ceiling.

The corpse disintegrated beneath the onslaught.

"Well," Ulysses commented, his voice tight. "*That's* a first."

"Did either of you recognize what he said?" I asked.

Ulysses gave me a wry look and then glanced at Gideon.

"The overall combination of dialects, yes," the other man said, surveying the ashes with his one good eye. "The words weren't quite right, though. Their translation is basically gibberish."

"That result sure as hell wasn't," Ulysses replied.

Gideon's brow shrugged.

I scowled, swiping water from my eyes. We were wasting time. Whatever the hell that bastard did, it wasn't nearly as important as making sure the girl didn't get away.

By the nurses' station, Doctor Sissoko gripped the desk as if it was the only thing keeping her standing.

"You okay, Doc?" Ulysses called.

She nodded jerkily.

I started for the hall again. "Security room," I ordered. "Doctor, stay with us."

She hurried to do just that.

The security station was a mess when we reached it. Half the monitors were on the floor and sprays of blood and dust were all that was left where the guards had been. Grimacing, Gideon stepped wide of the remains and tapped on the keyboard to wake the last surviving computer. The screen flickered to life.

"Cameras, cameras..." he muttered, scanning the interface. "There they are."

A few more clicks, and suddenly we could see a collection of camera feeds.

On every one of them, the halls were a swath of blood and destruction.

Doctor Sissoko made a nauseated sound.

"Where was the girl when you last saw her?" I asked Ulysses.

The man eyed me for a moment. "Southern wing," he said finally. "Hall B, heading west."

Gideon clicked through a few more commands. The views onscreen changed, switching through empty, bloody hall after empty, bloody hall.

"Dammit," I muttered.

"Can you rewind that thing?" Ulysses asked.

Gideon typed fast. Another angle came up, showing the length of the hallway. The recording scrolled back swiftly until we saw the rabid running in reverse along the length of the corridor.

"There!" The doctor pointed at the screen.

Gideon paused the recording and then hit play. At the end of the hall, Wren came into view by the door of the farthest room. At the sight of the rabid, she took off running down the corridor ahead of her, and the rabid charged after. Swiftly, Gideon switched to another camera, and then another, clicking through time stamps and tracking her as she ran.

Until she reached another door.

"South stairwell," Doctor Sissoko murmured, sounding worried.

"Where's it lead?" Ulysses asked.

"Vehicle shed."

Gideon clicked another control. The shed came into

view, and then the forest when Wren rushed for the outer exit.

She ran barefoot into the woods.

"Shit," I whispered to myself.

Gideon clicked through a few more commands, tracking her past the trees for a few more screens, before he leaned back from the desk. "That's it. No more cameras."

"Well, at least she's not dead," Ulysses offered and then paused. "Right?"

"You got an internet connection on this thing?" I asked Gideon rather than respond, twitching my chin at the computer.

He nodded.

"Find us an address for a Wren Cortwright. Search a fifty-mile radius. There can't be that many people with that name close by."

He nodded again and returned his attention to the computer.

Ulysses was watching me when I turned away. "I'm going to need some answers, Asher."

I avoided his gaze, glancing instead to Liam when the man appeared at the doorway. "How's it up there?"

He signed quickly. *Mostly intact. Elevator shaft's blown to hell.*

"You going to be all right here?" I asked the doctor.

"Yeah."

"Okay." I turned toward the door. "Then we need to head for—"

Ulysses stepped in front of me. "Screw that. You've

been weird since we found her. Now, either you tell me or we're staying put. What the hell's going on?"

I hesitated. By the door, Liam's eyebrow twitched up. I could feel Gideon watching me.

The doctor cleared her throat. "I'll just leave you four to…" She gave us an uncomfortable smile and fled the room.

"Why don't you want us near the girl, Asher?" Ulysses demanded. "Why watch her like a hawk for three damn nights?"

I looked away. I didn't want to tell them. I knew what it would do.

"What's bothering you, my friend?" Gideon's voice was low. "Because it's quite apparent something has you perplexed."

I scowled. "Right before the girl died, she… I felt something. She grabbed me, and she said 'Sentinel,' and —" I cursed silently. "It felt like the queen."

The room went so quiet, I could have heard the blood pumping through a gnat.

"What?" Gideon whispered.

Ulysses stepped away from me, shaking his head. "No. No, screw that." He scoffed. "That's not…" Still chuckling, he held up his hands as he retreated farther. "Not possible."

Gideon rubbed his palms back and forth across his thighs, nausea on his face. "Are you sure?"

"I—"

"Of course he's not sure!" Ulysses laughed. "He's imagining it. The girl's human, for gods' sakes—or she was. Hell, she doesn't even look like Amalie. There's no way—"

"I felt the bond."

Ulysses' fist slammed into a monitor. "The *fuck* you did!" His body trembled with tension, every trace of humor gone.

By the exit, Liam gripped the doorframe, his eyes locked on the floor like a thousand hells were opening up in front of him.

"We watched her die, Asher," Gideon said, his deep voice carefully controlled. "We *felt* her die, and the city burned when she did. I still hear the screams of the innocents she killed, and I know you do too. So I am asking you again." He drew a short breath. "Are. You. *Sure*?"

I couldn't meet his eyes. "I know what I felt."

Liam shoved away from the door, striding quickly from the room.

A cold scoff left Ulysses. "Maybe it was something else, you know? Maybe you just want it to be that."

I froze, hot rage boiling up through me like magma. "*What?*"

"You always were her favorite. Maybe you miss her after all these years."

Gideon moved fast, his arm catching me across the chest as I lunged toward Ulysses.

"Enough," Gideon snapped at him.

Fury twitched across Ulysses' face. "The bitch is dead, Asher. And fuck you for even *suggesting* she isn't."

Without another word, he stormed out of the room.

My muscles shook. Everything in me wanted to go after him, if only to beat the absolute shit out of him for daring to say that.

"He doesn't mean it."

"Like hell he doesn't," I snarled between clenched teeth, throwing Gideon a dark look.

The red-haired man grimaced, his brow drawing down over the leather patch covering his missing eye.

"I'd give anything for that bitch not to come back into this world, Gideon. Tell me you know that."

He hesitated, and nausea rolled inside me. I'd been a fool, centuries ago. A naive fool to believe that the queen's offer was a better bargain than the hangman's noose I faced for disobeying an order in the army I'd never wanted to join. And Ulysses wasn't wrong, as nauseating as the truth was. It had made me her favorite. The only one who'd chosen to be with her "willingly."

But that hadn't made being with her any less of a sentence in hell.

After a moment, though, Gideon nodded. "I do."

A breath left me. I knew he meant it. I even knew the words were true.

But I also knew we couldn't kill her. Not without killing us too. We'd damned ourselves centuries ago, tying our fate to hers, and only the gods knew how we'd escaped death the first time she'd died. But the four of us were all we each had left now, bound together by magic and blood, and I'd never sacrifice these men. Never truly hurt them—the occasional urge to pummel Ulysses aside.

And if she threatened them...

"But," Gideon continued quietly. "Barring the suicide that killing her would be, at least in theory... What do you want to do?"

I stepped away from him, raking a hand over my head.

"Find her. Lock her in a box buried a thousand feet beneath the earth and then... lose the key forever?"

He chuckled, but there wasn't much humor in the sound. "That *is* a plan." Sighing, he leaned back against the wall, crossing his arms. "Whatever these rabids want with her, we cannot let them take her. Especially since their actions make *no* sense."

My brow shrugged. That was an understatement. For pity's sake, they'd murdered her seven hundred years ago. And now...

"The girl may have gone to them," I said. "Running *just* when they attack like this...?"

"Suspicious."

"Very."

Gideon nodded. "Well, we have the address to where she's been staying, if nothing else. And she was heading west. It's possible she went to the house."

"We'll start in the forest. Work our way there. I don't want to miss the rabids if she's meeting them someplace."

He made a noise of agreement. I looked toward the exit, not moving.

Gideon sighed. "You visit the armory. I'll locate Ulysses and Liam." I gave him a wry look, and he shrugged. "Unless you want to waste time brawling?"

I chuckled. "Tempting."

He scoffed. "Go." His head twitched toward the door. "And know that I'm praying to the gods that you're wrong."

9

———————

WREN

*y feet should have been bleeding. I should have been cold. The ground was hard now. It hurt. But I should have been bleeding. There'd been a forest. Branches and rocks. I should...*

Blinking my bleary eyes, I stared at the lights in front of me for an eternity before the blare of a horn reached my ears. The lights veered away, and a blast of cold wind rocked me as the blur of a red pickup truck shot past my side.

And skidded to a stop.

A thunk followed. "Holy hell, girl! What're you doing out in the middle of the road like that?"

I winced as the glare of a flashlight hit my face, the beam lowering a moment later. A man in a flannel shirt peered at me.

"Wait, you're that—oh, my sweet Lord. Your momma and daddy have been looking for you!" He motioned to the truck. "Come back here, kid. You've got to be freezing. Let me grab my cell. I'll call you some help, okay?"

My eyes tracked him as he hurried back toward the driver's side of his truck. I felt... thin. Like my body was threadbare fabric stretched to the ripping point over my bones. I had no idea how long I'd been running. Hours, maybe? There'd been no trail. Just brambles and rocks and endless woods, lit up by silver that had to be the result of moonlight.

"Yeah. Out on Route Seven, about three miles north of Clarita Point." The man came back toward me, a gray blanket on his arm and his shoulder pinning his cell phone to his ear. His wide eyes watched me like I might bolt.

I felt like I could barely stand.

"I don't know. She—" The man bent slightly to catch my attention. "You hurt, girl?"

My head twitched back and forth.

"Doesn't seem like it," he told the person on the other end of the phone. "She's got on some weird hospital gown— Yeah, okay. You got it." He hung up and tried for a nervous smile as he shoved the phone into his pocket. "Cops are on their way. Squad car's only a mile or so on ahead of us." He chuckled. "You probably saved me from a speeding ticket."

I didn't know how to respond.

"Here." He unfurled the blanket and draped it around me. The scratchy fabric felt made of steel wool, and I cringed against it. "I'm not going to hurt you, girl. Let's just get you back to the truck where you can warm up, eh?" He motioned toward the pickup.

Shifting uncomfortably inside the blanket, I walked toward the vehicle. My nose twitched as I passed him, something strange tickling my senses, like a taste that was a smell that was...

Amazing.

I shuddered, my steps slowing. My eyes slid toward him, searching for the source of the smell-taste but it was everywhere. All over him. In fact, it *was* him, and yet...

My lips parted. The shuddering in my body grew stronger as my eyes locked on the ruddy skin of his neck past his flannel shirt. He had a tiny mustard stain on the collar like a constellation of yellow flecks, but that didn't matter. Even as I watched, I could see his skin twitching ever so faintly on the side of his throat, a steady rhythm that I could almost hear pulsing in my ears.

"Kid?" His voice was distant, lost beneath the growing beat. "Kid, you okay?"

A low growl rumbled in the back of my throat, unbidden. I turned toward him, my eyes locked on that tiny flinch of skin. It called to me, somehow promising an answer to what in the world I—

Lights flashed across my eyes. I recoiled, wincing in the glare with the weirdest feeling like I'd just snapped back to reality from someplace else.

Shivers crawled over my skin as if I were being swept beneath a tidal wave of ants. I felt off. Wrong. Weirder than I had since I left the clinic, and—

A low laugh interrupted my thoughts. I spun, but there was no one behind me. No one nearby at all, besides the guy staring like maybe I'd lost my mind. A cop car was rolling to a stop on the opposite side of the road from the pickup truck, but otherwise, the country highway was empty. The forest seemed that way too, each leaf and branch picked out by silver and hiding nothing.

But I'd heard somebody. A woman, I thought, chuckling like she was enjoying whatever she saw.

The thunk of a closing car door made me whirl again, my balance wobbling on my unsteady legs. The cop walked toward us, his stance cautious and his eyes scanning our surroundings as much as they did me.

"Wren Cortwright?" he called.

I couldn't seem to find the words to respond. My voice felt stuck to the inside of my throat. The cop glanced from me to the pickup truck driver and then motioned for me to go ahead of him. "I'm Sergeant Grisholm. You remember me from your mom's Christmas party two years back?" When I didn't respond, he continued. "I need you to get in my car. Do you understand? The captain is worried sick about you."

At my mom's title, I shivered, desperation rising up in me to just be *home*. In my bed at my parents' house. Maybe with a shower and everything of my childhood around me, familiar and safe and overwhelmingly *sane*. I nodded, hurrying toward the car as fast as my bare feet could carry me while the cop thanked the man from the pickup truck and then followed me toward the vehicle. Sergeant Grisholm held the door while I scrambled into the back, the hard seat slippery beneath my hands. As he shut the door, I looked back to see the pickup truck driver watching me, concern clear on his face.

I hugged my arms to my middle while the sergeant

climbed in and put the vehicle into gear. "C-can you tell me, um... How long have I been gone?"

He looked up at the rearview mirror, a guarded expression in his eyes. "It's been three days."

Shivering, I looked away as he pulled the car back onto the highway. The time didn't mean anything, whatever those people at that weird clinic said. I could've just been unconscious for three days, not dead.

My arms tightened. Beneath my grip, I could feel my pulse thudding in my veins.

I was fine.

Sergeant Grisholm took up his radio, informing someone on the other end that I was with him and we were heading back into town. A heartbeat later, the device squawked. "Captain Cortwright will meet you at Memorial Hospital."

"Understood," the sergeant replied.

I closed my eyes, my forehead resting on the cold surface of the window. Maybe when I opened my eyes again, I'd be in my bed and this would all have been a terrible dream.

Bright lights glared, making me flinch back as the car pulled to a stop. Memorial Hospital towered above me and the brilliant glow of the emergency room entrance was right beside me. Already doctors were hurrying out the door, one of them pushing a wheelchair ahead of them, while my mother raced alongside them.

A sob choked me. I yanked on the handle only to find it wouldn't open the door, but a moment later, the doctors tugged it wide anyway.

Child locks. Right. I scrambled out of the car, nearly falling on legs that seemed to have gone numb.

Hands grabbed me. Maneuvered me into the wheelchair. Voices swirled around me, asking me questions, gripping my arms or shoulders. From behind the sliding glass doors, I saw Harper and Dad come running toward me. My friends Brayden, Ollie, and Emma rushed after them.

And everyone was talking. Crying. Smiling and laughing with obvious relief and it was too much. I couldn't understand what they were saying. Couldn't even focus on the words because the blood was rushing in my ears, throbbing in an erratic beat like a dozen drummers were each making up a cadence of their own.

I was drowning in the rhythm and the rush. Darkness was encroaching on my vision, chewing away at the light while the drummers went mad in my head.

*Kill them.*

The whisper insinuated itself through the pounding, a woman's voice winding through my mind like a snake, and my heart raced at the sound. Gripping the armrests of the wheelchair, my hands trembled, my fingers curling toward claws.

*Bleed them. Flay them. Drink their blood as they scream and cry and—*

Cool hands took my cheeks. The whisper and the rampant pulsing died as my vision focused.

"Breathe, Wren." Harper crouched right in front of me. "Breathe."

I trembled, my gaze locking on my sister. Determination showed in her eyes, as if she would will the words into me, and tears glistened on her cheeks.

"You're safe now, okay? Whatever happened, it's over. You're safe."

Reaching up, I took one of her hands, gripping it hard as a ragged breath entered my lungs and my panic slowly drained. Harper smiled.

I nodded, hanging on to her and the words alike. Everything that came before this had been some mad delusion, and maybe those strange people had brainwashed me to boot, but now I was here. With my family. Back in the real world. And my sister was right.

Now, I was safe.

**10**

---

ULYSSES

That bitch would never take anyone I loved from me ever again.

Trembling from tension, I stood in the shadows beside a small house, watching the two-story colonial across the street. For hours, we'd swept the forest, scouring any area that looked like a hollow where rabids might hide, all for nothing. And this place was proving much the same. Various news vans were parked out front, with reporters and camera crews standing around as if they were just killing time. The windows of the house were dark, the curtains drawn. Even the porch light was off, and I couldn't see a car in the driveway.

Wherever the queen was, she hadn't come back here.

Unless, of course, that was the point. To look like she hadn't, to make these ridiculous humans camping out in front of a mid-class suburban home *think* she was some-where else.

Though why the hell she'd even been staying here...

I glared at the white siding and bright-blue shutters. Window boxes of multicolor flowers blossomed beneath the first-floor windows, and a wreath celebrating autumn hung on the door. None of it was her style. Gold trim was a minimum. Jewel-encrusted door knockers would have been required. The bitch hadn't slept on anything but handwoven silk sheets in all the centuries I'd known her, and she'd destroyed them as fast as the servants could bring them—sometimes by killing the servants.

This had to be a joke; I just couldn't find the punchline. The flowers. The cutesy decorations. Staying in something so common. So ordinary. So...

*"Uncle Ulysses! Uncle Ulysses!" Calliope ran up, a bouquet of weeds clutched in her little fist. Her chubby cheeks were flushed pink, and her dress was stained from grass and dirt. The evening sun glistened from her mahogany curls. "I found flowers for you!"*

I shuddered. I knew what came later that night: the swift and terrible attack out of nowhere. The blood. The screaming. The bitch vampire queen on her pale-white horse, staring down at me with a cold, cruel smile and demanding I serve at her side. I'd never seen her before that night. I'd never even believed vampires existed. To this day, I had no idea why she targeted *me*, out of all the people in the world.

But I remembered how she burned everyone I loved and everyone I knew when I dared to refuse her, until I begged her to stop and threw myself at her feet if only she would spare those few who were left.

And in the end, my desperate surrender saved only

one. Little Calliope, who ran in terror as the vampire bitch bit me. Who lived out her days a thousand years ago.

Whom I never saw again.

"It's been hours since the girl escaped," Gideon said over the earpiece. "If she'd come back here, I would have expected more activity from the humans."

"Unless she slipped past them," Asher countered.

I ground my teeth, forcing my attention back to the present. That bastard *never* should have kept something like this a secret. Not for one second, and certainly not for three fucking nights.

"The information I turned up on the internet claimed the girl's mother is a police captain," Gideon stated. "Perhaps she went to the station rather than—"

One of the news crews suddenly began shoving equipment in the back of their van.

"What the—" Gideon started.

Irritation filled me. I shifted to shadow immediately and took off across the street.

"Dammit, Ulysses," Asher hissed behind me.

Fuck him.

I landed behind a cluster of azalea bushes just in time.

"Memorial Hospital?" a reporter hissed to the van's driver, as if keeping his voice low so the other crews wouldn't hear. "They sure?"

"My cousin says she heard two orderlies talking. They've got the girl on overnight observation."

"Fantastic." The reporter glanced around. "Time and a half if you get us there ahead of anyone else."

The driver grinned. "Done."

My brow furrowed as the reporter circled the van and

then scrambled into the passenger seat. The queen was at a hospital? A *human* hospital, where they'd take her blood and possibly put her in a room with full sun? Sure, she'd just fed and if our bond to her was still active, the light wouldn't hurt her, but that still seemed a completely pointless risk. If humans took her blood, the government would find out about it, and then the GSS would be on their way.

Unless she was working with the government and their slayers? That still didn't make going to a hospital into a smart plan. But how else did I explain the quaint human neighborhood and the so-called mother who was a cop?

A chill rolled through me. Just when I thought things couldn't be any worse...

As the first van took off, the reporters from the rest scrambled to follow. Behind me, I heard a soft flutter.

"That was fucking reckless," Asher muttered.

I ignored him. "Girl's at the hospital."

An incredulous sound came from Gideon. "What?"

I strode toward the side of the house and launched into the sky while reporters sped away, chasing each other to get to their destination first.

They wouldn't beat me.

The others took to the air behind me, the sound of their passage so faint humans rarely ever heard. Asher would probably argue that we needed to act carefully. Gideon would want to think it through. But I knew Liam would understand. Amalie tortured him within an inch of his sanity and then destroyed his voice when she grew tired of his screams. He'd support me, no question.

Because I didn't care what it took. These men were my

family now. I'd do whatever was necessary to save them from her.

And I'd never go back to the hell the queen put us through. Maybe I couldn't attack her in front of the humans.

But, dammit, she wasn't going to be surrounded by humans forever.

**11**

———————

WREN

The silence was deafening.

Mostly because it was anything but quiet.

Lying on the hospital bed, I squeezed my eyes shut, but it only made things worse. The erratic rhythm around me had lessened since I'd first arrived, but it was by no means gone. If anything, it'd just become more bizarre, one beat loud and the rest rising and falling like random waves in the distance. I'd tried to drown the sound out with the television, but all that'd done was give me a headache. I'd tried a white noise app on my mother's phone, but it was just annoying. The noise was in my head, ceaseless, and with it droning on, I couldn't hope to sleep.

Grimacing, I shifted around on the bed and tried to lock my attention on the TV. Some old show about a cop with a dog was on, and God help me if I could follow the plot at all. Harper and Dad had gone home a few hours ago—someone needed to get the press out of there, my dad said, so I could come home to peace instead of mayhem—and my friends had left around the same time. Meanwhile, my mother was in the chair beside my bed, and somewhere between the dog chasing a bad guy and the cop bantering with another officer, she'd passed out.

The pounding rhythm was loudest toward her. I had no idea why.

A clack came from the window, like a tiny rock hitting the glass. I looked over sharply.

Nothing was there.

I drew the blanket up around me tighter. Of course there wasn't. It probably had just been a bug hitting the window, considering we were seven stories up. Outside the glass was a sheer drop to the parking lot.

I turned back to the television.

Four men stood at the foot of the bed.

I shrank back against the pillows, a scream dying in my throat. Asher and Ulysses I recognized, but the others were new. A giant of a man with a leather patch over one eye and a hooked scar circling the other. His red beard was grown long but still neatly shaped, and his hair was the color of rust, cut sheer on the sides and slightly longer on top. With his arms crossed in front of him, his enormous muscles bulging, his body seemed like a solid wall that would shatter me if I ran into it. Like the others, he bore an air of menace, and the look in his eyes utterly destroyed the entire hot mountain man image. Sharp like a knife. Incisive as one too. He watched me like I was a specimen in biology class that he was debating how to dissect.

*Gideon.*

I trembled, the sight of his naked body sweeping through my mind in a wave. His powerful muscles moved beneath his skin as he thrust himself into me. Sweat gleamed from his chest as I raked my nails across it, making him bleed. And more than that. The others too now, Asher, Ulysses, all of them together, touching me, pumping themselves into me as I writhed with pleasure between them.

And it felt so real. So unbelievably real.

My eyes flew to the other stranger of their own accord. Even among these men, he was distinct. Nearly as pale as an albino, with white-blond hair and ice-blue eyes, he looked like winter in human form, beautiful and deadly. He wasn't huge like Gideon. Everything about him was lean power, and each line of his body spoke of strength, clean and swift, like an icy wind ready to freeze the world. I shivered just to look at him.

The absolute hate in his eyes didn't help.

*Liam.*

Images of blood and the sound of screaming rose like a wave. The sight of him pinned, writhing as I rode him. Horror gripped me and gasping against sheer panic, I turned away, reaching for my mother. "Mom—"

She made a startled noise, jolting awake.

Liam was across the room before I got another word out, his fingers touching her forehead. She sagged back into the chair, her eyes closing again.

Terror shot through me. I grabbed for the alarm button, but Ulysses snagged me immediately, wrenching my wrist around. I shrieked as pain lanced through my arm, but his other hand clamped over my lips, trapping the sound. Gone was the friendly, cocksure smile I'd seen when I first met him. Now, he looked like he'd skin me alive and enjoy every second.

My eyes darted around, praying someone would come in.

And kind of petrified for what these men would do if anyone did.

Darkness swept through in my mind, snakelike shadows coursing through my body and down my arms at the speed of thought. A snarl rose in my chest, unbidden, totally out of my control, carrying words that weren't my own.

*My possessions shouldn't do such things.*

Ulysses released me, recoiling with his eyes wide, a glistening knife suddenly in his fist.

I couldn't even scream. My mouth felt like it wasn't my own, like something else was moving in my skin, trying to take command of my muscles.

"Did—" Ulysses started, his face half-turned toward the others and his eyes locked on me. "Did you feel—"

My panic finally broke through the suffocating sensation gripping my throat. "Help! Somebody, please—"

Liam lunged at me with a raspy cry. His hands drove me back as his mouth went for my throat.

I shrieked, shoving at him, and a surge of strength rolled through me. He flew backward, staggering into the wall and catching himself there.

"Shit!" Ulysses cried.

"Please," I tried. "Please, I don't know what you—"

The darkness in my mind swelled like a monster rising from the deep, fury pouring from it in a cascade. But it wasn't me. Nothing I recognized at all. And as much as it wanted to punish the men, it wanted me utterly destroyed.

It *hated* me. Even as it poured through my limbs, through my throat, it wanted to burn me to ash, leaving nothing but an empty shell.

I screamed.

The darkness snarled, recoiling from the sound. Seething with rage, it fell back and sank into the recesses of my mind.

I opened my eyes. I was still on the hospital bed, my hands clamped against the sides of my head and my legs drawn up like a child hiding from a nightmare.

And the men were staring at me.

"What the fuck?" Ulysses whispered.

I looked around in the hope my mother would have woken or a nurse would be breaking down the door. But there was nothing. Just me, trapped in this room with unspeakably hot men.

Who all wanted to kill me.

Asher glanced at the others. "You felt that, yes? As if she…"

"Fought it off," Gideon finished.

Liam pushed away from the wall carefully, not taking his eyes from me.

I trembled. "Who are you? Why are you here?"

Ulysses scoffed, but he sounded more taken aback than contemptuous, like I was confusing the hell out of him more and more with each passing second. "No way. This is some trick, man. It's bullshit."

"Put the knife away, Ulysses," Asher said, his focus still locked on me.

"The hell I will."

"You're scaring the girl."

"Pretty sure that's the idea."

Asher's jaw muscles jumped. "Humans checked you out, didn't they?" he said to me. "Did they take your blood?"

I didn't respond. The way they were watching me had changed, from utter hate to something far more cautious. And a new thought suddenly passed through my mind to see them each staring at me like I'd suddenly transformed into a two-headed cobra.

Were these men *scared* of me?

"Answer the question." Gideon tossed the words at me like a challenge.

Anger bubbled up inside me on the heels of the realization. "You first."

Ulysses took a step forward with the knife. "Do not fuck with us, girl. You—"

"Fine," I snapped. "Yes."

Asher scrubbed a hand over his head. "Dammit."

"What does that matter?" I demanded.

Now they looked at me like I was terrifying *and* stupid.

Gideon shook his head slowly. "What is going *on*?"

My brow rose. "What are you talking about? You're the ones who broke in here."

Asher threw a glance at the others and then took a step toward me. I recoiled on the bed. "Any minute now, a group of government officials will be coming in here to kill you, do you understand?"

"Um... no?" I cast a quick glance at the door, wondering where the nurses were because surely one of them heard me screaming. "Look, I don't know who you are, but if you just leave me alone, I swear I won't tell anybody—"

"You sure she isn't working with them?" Ulysses demanded of Asher.

I sputtered. "I don't know who you're talking—"

Ulysses pointed the knife at me. "Keep lying, bitch. We've learned a few things since our time with you. You want us to try them out?"

I stared at him.

"If she's working with the GSS, she wouldn't have come here," Asher said. "Too much risk of exposure."

Ulysses turned away, his jaw muscles jumping.

"We take her with us," Gideon said.

"*What*?" Ulysses cried.

A protesting noise left me. "I'm not going anywhere with you."

"You felt the queen," Gideon continued to the others, ignoring me. "She's inside this... girl." He said the word like I was a bug. "We cannot leave her to be captured by rabids or killed by the GSS. We need answers and interrogating her is the only way we'll get them."

"Hey, I said I'm not going anywhere! You can't just—"

Asher crossed to the side of the bed, while behind him, the others made alarmed noises. "The GSS are the Government-Sanctioned Slayers. They kill any vampire who has been turned without authorization. And if you're not working with them, then that means you're their target now. So either you come with us and maybe you'll live, or you stay here and you'll be a pile of dust on that bed before the sun rises."

My mouth moved.

"They'll tell your family you were kidnapped, or maybe that you ran away, and then in a few weeks, they'll turn up a burned body they'll claim is yours. Your family will have a funeral, and they'll all be very sad, but then everyone will go on with their lives. Except you."

I shook my head. "I'm not... I wasn't turned into a... I'm just a person. I'm not..."

The men stared at me, incredulous.

Liam's attention suddenly snapped to the side, alarm on his face. Quickly, he opened the door a crack, peering into the hallway and then retreating fast. In swift sign language, he told something to the others. I couldn't understand a word of it, but the tension in his motions was easy enough to comprehend.

Something was really wrong.

From beyond the closed door, I could hear the faint murmur of voices, their words unintelligible.

Gideon muttered something that, even if I didn't know the language, certainly had to be a swear word. "If they brought a wraith and some shifters, they might know we're here. What now?"

"We leave," Ulysses snapped. "Fuck this."

"Take her." Asher nodded to me, his eyes on Gideon. "We'll figure it out when—"

The door shattered inward, chunks of wood flying everywhere. Through the gap, two people rushed in. Dressed in suits like agents from *Men in Black*, they hurled something ahead of them as they barreled through the opening. Glass shattered against Ulysses and Liam, and the men recoiled, smoke rising from them. Three other people raced through the door, throwing more things, sending Asher and Gideon retreating.

"I'm not with them!" I shouted.

Nobody cared. Without hesitation, one of the newcomers lunged at me, a wooden stake suddenly sliding from her sleeve. Catching it effortlessly, she swung at me.

I shrieked, scrambling sideways on the bed and then toppling to the tile floor.

The stake slammed down, ripping through the pillow right where I'd been. Frantic, I shoved to my feet. Asher and the others were fighting the attackers, blood hitting the walls as the four men landed blows with their knives. Suddenly, one of the suit-clad people snarled, his eyes turning to black pits, his cheeks sinking into his skull, and his skin going deathly white. Lunging through the air, he slammed into Ulysses.

"Liam!" Asher shouted.

Swiftly, Liam leapt at the creature, turning to shadow mid-jump. Ripping the thing away from Ulysses, he tangled around the attacker, who slashed at him with hands that seemed more like claws.

The woman who tried to stab me ripped the spike from the pillow and then scrambled over the mattress like a human spider, still coming for me.

I looked around, frantic, but there was nowhere to go. I was pinned in the corner. Beyond the bed, my mother was still slumped in her chair, her chest rising and falling steadily, utterly undisturbed by the fighting all around her. But where were the nurses? Where were the orderlies? All hell was breaking loose in here, and—

"Gideon!" Asher shouted. "Grab the girl!"

The red-haired man shoved back a guy who looked like a Neanderthal and cast a fast glance at me. The woman with the stake snarled, and as Gideon lunged toward me, she hurled the wooden spike through the air.

Shadows engulfed me, ripping me to the side. The wood impaled itself in the plaster wall right where I'd been. Lifting me up, the shadows didn't stop.

Glass shattered. Cold wind bit at me like a thousand tiny teeth.

Oh my God, we'd gone out the window.

Eyes wide, I looked around fast. We weren't falling. Certain death—aka the ground—stayed the same distance from me as it had been. And instead of plummeting to my doom, I was racing through the air with nothing but darkness enfolding me, surrounded by the sound of a cape flapping in the wind. Receding behind me, the broken window of the hospital gaped in the night, and through it, I could still see the others fighting.

One of the attackers bent over my mother.

I thrashed in the shadow's grip, shouting for her. In spite of everything, she still hadn't woken up, and now—

"They won't hurt her." Gideon's gravelly voice was right at my ear.

From the window, Asher and Ulysses leapt into the night, turning to shadows that raced across the sky. A moment later, another shadow followed. Liam, I hoped.

Rather than anything else.

I trembled. Somewhere in the past minute or so, the four terrifying men who possibly wanted me dead had become a better option than the stake-wielding people in suits who *definitely* did.

The hospital receded from view, and then the town beneath me did as well. The shadow holding me raced above the fields beyond the city limit until, when a forest passed below us, it changed direction. My stomach hit my throat as Gideon dove toward a clearing, and when we reached the ground, he let me go so quickly that I tumbled on the grass and rocks. Darkness seemed to fall back from him like he was stepping from a black fog, only to fold into him like a cloak vanishing at his back, leaving him standing in front of me, eye patch and military garb in place.

The other three landed beside him, shifting back to human form as well.

Warily, I pushed to my feet, drawing myself up as tall as I could and forcing a defiant look onto my face. I was alone in a forest, barefoot and wearing only a hospital gown in front of four men whose bodies I somehow knew intimately. But by God, I wouldn't cower.

No matter how much part of me inside was screaming.

"Anybody follow?" Gideon asked.

Asher shook his head. "Shifters backed down once you took the girl. The rest were just amped-up humans." He paused. "And Liam killed the wraith."

"Oh, the GSS is going to love us for that," Ulysses commented.

None of the others responded.

"What the hell are they going to do to my mother?" I demanded.

"Nothing," Gideon said. "As I told you."

"The GSS won't harm a human as long as that human doesn't try to stop them with their mission," Asher added. "That's their mandate. You're not there anymore, so they'll simply test her, and when she doesn't react like a vampire, they'll let her go."

I swallowed hard. There were a lot of unspoken *ifs* in that statement, not the least of which was the assumption Mom wouldn't try to stop them. And if she did, even by accident?

"What about the part..." My stomach churned at the thought. "The part about them claiming I was kidnapped? Or dead? My family was already terrified enough for me these past few days. I can't just leave them thinking I'm..." I couldn't even find the words.

Asher and Gideon glanced at each other, while Ulysses still bore an expression of contempt, as if surely I was playing some sort of trick. Meanwhile, Liam watched me like he'd never quite seen anything like me before in his life.

"With a secure line, I could arrange a phone call," Gideon said as if answering some unspoken question from Asher.

"Oh, no. You're not bringing her back to the manor." Ulysses shook his head. "I'll burn that shit to the ground before I let her step foot in there."

I glared at him.

He ignored me completely, scoffing at Asher's exasperated expression. "What? You know this has got to be some game of hers. She's *playing* with us, and I'm not—"

"Hey!" I snapped. "I'm right here. Stop talking about me like I'm not even—"

Ulysses spun toward me, hurling a knife through the air. It impaled itself in the ground only an inch from my toes. "You don't speak again."

I shuddered hard, staring at him. The challenge in his eyes was so clear, I could read it without even trying.

If I went for the knife, he'd kill me.

I turned, walking toward the edge of the clearing away from them.

"Dammit," Asher swore behind me.

My bare feet moved faster over the rough ground. I was done. I didn't care what was happening, how these people could turn into shadows, or why monsters had broken into my hospital room. I was done, and going home, and—

A hand snagged my shoulder. I shrieked, trying to rip away from it.

I might as well have tried to break stone.

"You go out there, you're going to die," he said.

A raw noise left me. "Why do you care? You tried to kill me too! No, I'm going home. I'm not a vampire; I'm not anything. I'm just going home and you—"

He spun me toward him, catching both of my shoulders. Inside me, the darkness stirred and frantically, I bashed it back as hard as I could.

His eyes narrowed. "How are you doing that?"

"Let me *go!*"

"We can't."

I yanked at his grip harder. He grunted, hanging on. "Why?" I demanded.

"Because if you die, we could too."

I stopped. "What?"

"Way to give away the farm, Asher," Ulysses muttered, making a quick grabbing gesture. Where it stuck up from the ground, his knife vanished like reality had simply swallowed it whole.

I blinked, my mind adding that to the pile of "stuff that couldn't be happening."

Asher looked over his shoulder at him. "If this is a trick, she already knows what could happen to us. And if it's not, I'd prefer she know what she's risking—for your damn sake *and* mine."

My mouth moved. How the hell was I supposed to take that? If I died, they died. That didn't make the least bit of sense.

"The witch could help us settle all of this," Gideon offered into the silence.

I looked past Asher to him, alarmed. "Witch?"

Ulysses scoffed. "You think she's going to talk to us after Chicago?"

Liam signed something.

"Yeah..." Ulysses replied. "Don't think she owes us *this* much." He gestured toward me.

I tried to back away from Asher. "Not to sound like a broken record here, but I'm not going anywhere except home."

His grip didn't budge. "The GSS *will* find you there. They will kill you and anyone who gets in their way."

Air pressed from my chest.

"Gideon's right," Asher continued to the others. "We see the witch. We get our answers." His eyes returned to me. "And hopefully you'll get some too."

I looked away.

"If nothing else," he added in a lower voice. "It'll make Ulysses—and all of us—more comfortable about bringing you to where you could use one of our phones."

My eyes flicked back to him, and I was aware on some level that I was essentially bargaining with kidnappers.

Ones who'd sort of saved my life. "Okay."

Behind me, Ulysses made a disgusted noise. "Fine. We're off to see the witch. Just don't blame me when she turns us all into toads."

**12**

———

WREN

The men-who-were-shadows set down several miles farther into the forest, and if life hadn't been strange enough, now I'd fallen straight into some kind of wicked-witch fairy tale.

A run-down cabin sat beneath the trees, the entire building nearly lost beneath a carpet of ivy and moss. Gold light spilled through a single curtained window to shine out on the night, glinting from the countless baubles and ornaments made of shattered glass that dangled from tree limbs all around. A winding track lined by odd-shaped stones led up to the porch, while overgrown gardens filled the space on either side.

Yup. We were going to meet someone with *serious* delusions they were a wicked witch, all right. Or else who hadn't seen civilization for a few dozen years.

Though, given the fact I was being flown around by guys who could become shadows...

I shoved the thought aside. I wasn't a vampire, this

woman wouldn't be a witch, and the sooner I got this over with, the sooner I could get in touch with my family and let them know I was okay.

I started toward the house. A startled noise left Gideon, and then the men hurried after me.

"Careful," Asher said, his voice low. "Traps."

My feet slowed. Right. Of course.

The men stopped shy of the porch, and Gideon cleared his throat. "Eden? We mean no harm. May we enter?"

A moment passed.

"Yeah," Ulysses muttered. "Great plan. This is—"

The door opened.

I blinked. Given the surroundings, I'd expected an old lady. Maybe somebody with warts or a serious issue with bathing. Instead, a slender young woman with long light-brown hair stood at the door wearing jeans and a t-shirt for a local band.

"Blowing up my house in Chicago not good enough for you boys?" Her voice was sharp, without a trace of discomfort for telling off four guys who probably towered over her by a foot.

"Again," Asher said. "We're sorry about that."

Her jaw worked around. "Uh-huh." Her eyes flicked to me, and she paused. A chuckle left her. "Though I see what brought you."

I struggled not to retreat, suddenly wary, and more than a bit self-conscious to be standing here, barefoot, in a hospital gown.

For a moment longer, she studied us all and then nodded toward the house. "Come on inside." She held up a hand with a warning expression. "But if I lose this house too? You're going to be eating flies for a century, got it?"

Asher and Liam nodded, and even Ulysses looked chagrined.

"Yes, ma'am," Gideon murmured.

The witch's lip twitched, and her attention turned back to me. "I'm Eden, by the way. It's nice to meet you, Wren."

I faltered. "H-how did you know my name?"

"Oh, you created quite the disturbance when you woke to your new life. The guys here don't know the half of it." She grinned. "And I'm friends with Mariam, your doctor from the clinic. She asked me to keep an eye out for you... my way."

Winking at me, she turned and walked back to the door, holding it aside while I trailed the others in. Scents bombarded me when I passed the threshold— pine and lemon, flowers and cinnamon, all rioting around one another, vying for prominence. Drying plants hung from all the rafters, and at the far end of the room, a pot bubbled on the stove. To my right, a small staircase led up to a loft that overlooked the room; past the railing there, I could see the edge of a mattress covered in mismatched quilts and crocheted blankets. To my left, a fireplace stood, no flames inside but a pot hanging above where they would be. Knickknacks covered the mantle—crystals, bones, a ball of thread, and several carvings shaped like animals—all surrounding sepia-toned pictures of people in pioneer garb. But in the center of the room, a table stood, an evergreen cloth draped over the top and a large bowl of blue-glazed pottery sitting in the middle. More bones and crystals surrounded that, along with a silver knife on one side and a pair of glistening scissors on the other.

My feet slowed. "What, um… what's all that for?"

Eden smiled, and she could've given the *Mona Lisa* a run for her money. I had no idea how to read the expression, but when she glanced up at me, a chill ran through me all the same.

"So, what did they say to get you here?" she asked me.

"I want to know that my family is safe, and they won't let me get a phone call until we talk to you."

Eden gave the men a wry look. "Keeping prisoners now, are we?"

"We just want to know what we're dealing with first," Asher said.

"An innocent."

Ulysses scoffed. "Right."

I gave him a wary glance, but the witch just chuckled.

"Very well. Allow me to show you." Eden took the pair of scissors from among the knickknacks on the table. "May I?"

I gave her a wary look. "May you what?"

"I need a lock of your hair. Doesn't have to be much. If you don't mind? Willing contributions are best."

Blinking at her, I wasn't sure whether to laugh. The wicked witch wanted some of my hair. Nothing to worry about here. "Um, sure."

She snipped a few strands away so quickly, she was done by the time I realized what she was doing. Turning, she walked back to the far end of the table and murmured something under her breath before casting the strands into the bowl.

In spite of myself, I craned my neck a bit to see what was happening. The large clay bowl held dark liquid, the bottom impossible to see past it. Holding her hands over the surface, the woman continued murmuring to herself, and I couldn't make out the words.

But the hairs on my arms stood on end.

Swiftly, she snagged items from the table and cast them into the bowl in rapid succession, a focus to her motions like each object was a deliberate choice.

The bones and crystals passed into the liquid without even a ripple. A glow began to blossom inside the bowl, like a tangle of light spiraling bigger and brighter with every passing moment. Smoke rose, twisting like a shimmering aurora over the dark surface. In the reflection, shapes formed.

I gasped. I could see my mother as if I was watching her on TV. Amid the glow, Mom was yelling at a nurse at the hospital and gesturing to the room over her shoulder. I recognized the number. It was my hospital room, except the door was intact.

"Is this—"

"This is now," Eden answered my breathless question. Her hands moved, and she murmured low words.

Sound reached my ears. "—do you mean you don't know where she's gone?" Fury colored my mother's voice, but I could hear the thread of panic beneath it too, and it made my heart hurt. She was scared for me.

Again.

The image shifted. My father ran into the building, the

sliding glass doors of the hospital only barely making it out of his way in time, and Harper was on his heels. They raced past the front desk, ignoring the young man who called out that visiting hours were over. When he reached the elevator, Dad jabbed the button over and over, muttering curses under his breath.

"They're going to tell them I'm dead, aren't they?" I whispered. "Those government people. They're going to do what you said."

I looked to the men. Asher appeared uncomfortable, while Gideon eyed me like I was a curious bug and Liam watched me like I was a strange, possibly dangerous creature.

Ulysses just glared.

I ignored the others, focusing on Asher. "I have to tell my family I'm okay. Please." When he said nothing, I turned to the witch. "Do you have a phone?"

She hesitated. "There was another question," she said rather than answer, her attention sliding to the men.

"Who is this girl?" Gideon asked immediately.

Eden smiled. Returning her focus to the strange liquid in the bowl, she began chanting again. The swirls rose again, different this time. Dark red like blood, but glowing. Around me, it felt like electricity began to build, as if I was standing at ground zero of a lightning strike.

The witch looked up.

I froze. Her eyes were clouded white, her irises and the pupils totally gone, and I had the strangest feeling that she was not only looking at me, but straight through me as well. Her hair stirred as if in a breeze, and yet the air in the room was entirely still.

"I see you," she intoned. Her voice seemed to reverberate in my chest, but even though her cloudy eyes were locked on me, it didn't feel like she was speaking to me at all.

Whispers rose in my mind. Goose bumps rose on my arms as shivers coursed through my body.

"Mote of the queen," Eden continued. "Clinging to life and the soul that once was her own. Leech from the past. You have no place here."

Nervousness quivered in my chest.

Eden's lips curled in an enigmatic smile below her clouded eyes. Extending her hands over the bowl, she began to chant words in a language I didn't recognize.

The trembling grew worse. My skin crawled and nausea twisted my stomach. But then the sensation began to recede, as if my awareness of my own body was drifting back, floating free, tethered to my flesh only like a balloon on a string, and darkness poured like black ink into the space I'd left. I could almost see it, like I was watching my own body from a distance as a sentient shadow poured through my muscles.

My hand moved, but not of my own free will. Striking the bowl hard, I sent the vessel flying from the table, where the pottery shattered against the ground. Liquid splashed everywhere, and Eden stumbled back.

A laugh rumbled up in my chest. I didn't recognize the sound, but I couldn't stop it. Couldn't do anything more than float here, watching, attached only by a thread that would break at any moment.

Eden threw out a hand at me, shouting something that wasn't in English.

I snapped back into my own body, stumbling hard and reeling as if I'd been gut-punched.

"Don't!" Eden snapped.

Knives in their hands, the men froze.

I couldn't even retreat. I was too busy trying not to scream at the darkness still twisting around inside me like a snake trying to evade being caught.

Moving fast, Eden snagged something from the table. I caught a flash of silver chain, and then she looped it over my head and around my throat.

Alarmed, I looked down. A pendant hung from my neck, a strangely metallic-looking stone that glinted with myriad colors in the dim light. Wrapped in intricate twists of metal, it hung just above my breasts from a chain of tiny silver links.

But immediately, the darkness inside my mind began to recede, and a weight I hadn't even realized I'd been carrying seemed to lift from my muscles.

For a moment, no one moved.

"What... the *fuck*," Ulysses whispered. His grip adjusted on the knife like he still wasn't sure he shouldn't use it.

"This one is not your enemy," Eden said.

The skepticism at her statement was palpable. On some level, I even shared it.

Drawing a breath, Eden pushed her hair away from her face. "The charm will reduce the queen's impact for a time, but she is not gone. *However*"—she put a hand up at Ulysses when he started forward again—"this girl is not the queen. She is the queen's soul reborn."

"And that's *better*?" Ulysses demanded.

"What does that mean?" Asher asked, incredulous.

Eden smiled. "What I said. When someone is reborn, their soul returns to a state of endless possibility. Whatever they may have been in a past life, this time they have the opportunity to be different. To do more or make better choices. But occasionally, the past still tries to hang on, carrying through the ether between life and death, trailing behind them, neither alive nor dead, but simply an echo of what was. Sometimes, this is essentially harmless, or it can even be enlightening. But other times, it can be toxic. And if strong enough or given enough power..." She glanced at me, pity in her eyes. "It can be deadly."

I trembled.

Taking a breath, Eden splayed her hands on the table. "Given the strength of what you're facing, I doubt this was brought about merely by the former queen alone. Someone has a modicum of the old queen still in this world, gaining strength over the centuries. Perhaps a bone or some other relic from that lifetime."

"Her body burned," Asher said, his voice tight. "All of it."

"And yet you did not die. Surely, it occurred to you something of her may have survived."

Asher looked away.

"Whatever remains," Eden continued. "That mote of self wishes to lay claim to her reborn soul and oust Wren from this body, so that the old queen might live again. It is that which you all felt earlier. It is that"—her eyes locked on me—"which you hear in your mind as she tries to take command of your body."

I shook my head. "That's not possible. That's not

even..." I looked at the men, but they all seemed guarded or shell-shocked in turns. "This can't be real."

"The old queen seeks to destroy you." Eden's voice was implacable. "And if she does, she will claim your body, allowing her to regain all her power to use across what would have been your own lifespan—one that, now that you've been turned, could extend for centuries or more. The hell she could wreak then would be unspeakable. Thousands of dead. Cities and nations burned to the ground with mountains of corpses left in her wake. And if you doubt me, ask them what the cost was last time she lived." She nodded toward the men, not taking her eyes from me. "Ask them how many innocents perished, both before and *when* she died."

Still shaking my head, I backed away from the table. "I'm just me, okay? I'm not—"

"You are the reborn soul of Amalie von Morgenstierne, called the Desolation, the Bloodwright, the Artist of Death, and the Mistress of Hell. Queen of the Vampires."

Deep inside, I felt the darkness stir as if recognizing its own name.

"In your past life, these four men were bound to you. The Sentinels. Your bodyguards and much more, sworn to your side, charged through blood magic to die as well if you perished. Somehow, they escaped that fate"—she gave a pointed look to Asher and the others—"but if the queen returns, she'll reclaim that bond. She'll force them back into servitude, and she will gladly kill you and all you hold dear." Eden's voice was low and intense, and her eyes were like augers drilling into my soul. I suddenly knew without a shadow of a doubt that, no matter how young she looked, I was in the presence of someone who had seen the passing of centuries.

And from the look of it, had watched them burn.

"If you mean to survive," she told me. "You will have to do more than embrace that old bond. You will have to cast it anew. Claim your power. Join with these men in *this* life and strengthen the ties between all of you so that she cannot overcome them. Otherwise, she will steal your life from you and use it to rain hell on all the earth."

My head shook. I could feel the pressure of the men's eyes on me like burning brands on my skin. "I don't—"

"Whatever you were prior to being turned, Wren, now you have a calling no one but you can fulfill. The vampires are depending on you to save them from Amalie. We all are. You must accept what has happened. You *must* let go of your denial and embrace your new destiny. If you don't, she will kill you."

I couldn't speak. I was trembling too hard.

Eden stepped back, turning her gaze on the four men around me. "You guarded the queen once, despite all your torment, and at that time, you had no choice. You have one now, though it is not without cost. Protect this girl because even though she is the reborn soul of your torturer, she is also an innocent. Or abandon her and know that the forces seeking to bring the queen back will surely claim her." The witch paused. "I know your bond is still there. I can see it, weak and damaged between all of you. What you choose to do with it will determine not only your fate, but all of ours as well."

From the corner of my eye, I could see the men turn toward me. In the distant recesses of my mind, the darkness stirred, muttering vicious imprecations I couldn't understand.

My head shook as if to deny the darkness or maybe even this place.

Because this was insane. It *had* to be insane. Wasn't the old cliché that everyone in the mental institution thought they were Napoleon? And now... what? I was supposed to accept, on the word of a stranger, that I was a reborn *vampire queen*? A homicidal one, at that?

This had to be a joke. It had to be—

"Wren," Asher said quietly.

I bolted from the room.

# 13

WREN

I didn't make it five feet from the door before they followed me.

"Wren," Gideon called. "We must discuss this. You cannot—"

"Leave me alone!" I didn't stop. I had no idea where I was in this goddamn forest, but this wasn't exactly the Alaskan wilderness. A road would be out there somewhere, and with it, a way home.

"I realize this is a lot to take in," Asher began.

"Oh, do you?" I whirled, glaring. Behind him, the others watched me like I might turn into a hydra or maybe just strike them dead like a god.

I scoffed. "Complete lunacy is 'a lot to take in'? How about it's *batshit*! I'm not—"

"Have you felt the bond?" he persisted.

Asher's eyes were so intent on mine that I had to look away.

"I haven't felt jack, okay?" The lie tasted sour in my

mouth, but I pressed on. "Nothing. I don't..." I struggled to regroup, starting back down the path again. "I don't know you. Any of you. And this is just... No."

Gideon suddenly appeared in front of me, shifting from shadow to human form. "The queen *cannot* be allowed to return. No matter the cost. She must—"

"Enough!" I shrieked. "Look, I don't know what the *hell* you guys are, what Eden is, or anything at all. But it's not my problem. I—"

"Not your *problem*?" Ulysses exclaimed.

"No!" I steered wide of Gideon and kept moving. "I'm not some ancient queen, okay? I'm an ordinary person who is *done*. I don't want any part of—"

"Oh, fuck this," Ulysses snapped behind me.

I turned back to see him striding toward me.

"You want to know why it's your problem?" he demanded. "You want to know why we have to stop this?"

"Wait," Gideon protested. "What are you—"

"Don't!" Asher shouted.

Ulysses' hands gripped the sides of my head.

A different reality hit me like a wall. Images didn't just flash through my mind, they engulfed it, stealing every sense, wiping out the forest and all the world. Blood poured over my naked skin, hot and viscous, smelling of iron and drained from a thousand victims whose city was burning beyond my windows. Servants screamed while I watched them skinned alive. Embers danced on the air, while pyres of corpses lit up the night sky until it glowed like midday.

More images, then. Faster. Blood coating the floors and

dead bodies hanging from the rafters and the howls of victims ringing out into the night. Sex and torture, intricately intertwined. Inseparable and beautiful and, gods, I could never get enough. These men, four beautiful men, so noble and unbroken, even as their bodies lay bloodied beneath me. And no matter the suffering, I knew they'd still rise. Still come to my call because I gave them no choice.

Gideon thrashing in chains, his bloodied socket gaping emptily after I ripped out his eye.

Ulysses howling in torment, surrounded by the bodies of people he loved, the people I'd slaughtered before binding him to me forever.

Liam lashed to the bed, his body nothing but ribbons of flesh coated in blood, his beautiful voice silenced for eternity.

Asher, his soul dying in his eyes as I forced him to fuck me until I screamed on sheets still wet with the blood of those he'd sworn to protect—

The images shattered as I crashed to the ground. Horror rolled through me, and I gagged, my insides heaving as though to vomit out my soul, though nothing but stomach acid came up. My ears still rang with the howls of the dying, and I could barely see the grass beneath me. Sobs choked me. I couldn't breathe. Somewhere, somehow, the dead were still screaming.

And then I realized it was just me.

I crumpled in on myself, shrieking against the nightmares still playing out behind my eyes. In the distance, I heard shouting and a crash like the sound of a fight, but I couldn't look. Didn't want to see. Tears tasted like salt in my mouth as I sobbed until my chest ached, but I couldn't make myself stop.

Because, oh my God, why hadn't I stopped? Why had I ever, *ever* done such horrible—

Firm hands scooped me from the earth, and then a cool sensation swallowed me as the ground fell away. Wind rushed past with the sense of gravity losing its grip. I was flying again. One of them had me. I couldn't see at all, didn't even want to open my eyes, and for a dark moment I wondered if they'd lifted me into the sky simply to let me fall.

But the sensation of being held tight never faltered, and after a small eternity, the grip of gravity changed as we descended once more. A click followed, and then the air seemed to shift, drawing closer, becoming filled with the scents of lavender and polished wood.

I sank into something soft as the cool feeling pulled back. Golden light glowed from stained-glass Tiffany lamps in the room around me. I lay on a four-poster bed, a white comforter under me and pillows beneath my head.

Liam stood at my side, nothing but sorrow on his face.

At the sight of him, a sob choked me, images flashing through my mind so powerfully, I could see the blood on him even as he stood in front of me, untouched. His screams rang in my ears, and I curled into a fetal position on the bed, squeezing my eyes shut in a desperate attempt to escape the horror.

But Liam didn't lash out. Didn't attack or hurt me. Instead, a soft blanket draped over my body and then quiet footsteps moved away. Biting my lip against a sob, I peeked my eyes open warily to see him walking to the window, where he closed and locked it before continuing to the door. Pulling it back only a bit, he motioned to someone outside the room and then sealed it shut again.

I trembled beneath the blanket. What was he doing?

But he only sighed as he sank down to the ground. Crossing his legs beneath him, he leaned back against the door and turned his attention to the window, something so watchful in his gaze.

Like a bodyguard.

An unsteady breath left me. I had no idea where we were or what he meant by bringing me to this place, yet even if it made no sense given everything I'd done to him, I was still grateful. Somehow, I felt safe here.

Safe... but also ashamed.

I closed my eyes, tears soaking into the pillow as I cried.

**14**

---

ASHER

I couldn't get to Wren fast enough.

But I'd be damned if I'd let Ulysses keep hurting her.

Slamming into him, I ripped him away from Wren, my body turning to shadow immediately and tangling around him, restraining him. He shouted curses at me and then shifted form too, thrashing hard enough to break my grip. Surging away from me, he started toward her again. In an instant, Gideon appeared, snaring him, and I lunged forward to help. We tumbled, breaking through Eden's garden, crashing across the bushes and flowerpots.

There'd be hell to pay with the witch, but right at this moment, I didn't really care.

Wren's screams cut like a knife, the sound tortured and horrifying. Cries like I heard in my nightmares, rising from ancient memory of all the hell the queen wrought. Rage poured through me to hear them now, and I plowed into Ulysses, driving him toward the edge of the woods.

Her screams faded. I spun in time to see a shadow vanishing against the night sky. Gideon stood in the garden, watching them go.

Liam was nowhere to be seen.

Ulysses started after them. Rushing upward, I snagged him and hurled him back to the ground.

He crashed into the garden and then shifted form, glaring up at me. I landed fast, changing shape too.

"You son of a bitch!" I snapped. "You could've killed her!"

Seething, he made no move to get up from the garden. "Maybe that's what it takes. Maybe if she's dead, the queen can't—"

Gideon made an aghast noise. "I hope to the *gods* you're not this far gone, brother. I'm not saying we should trust the girl, but *killing* her—"

"Dammit," I snapped. "Eden said she was an innocent."

"How do we know that for sure, huh?" Ulysses retorted.

"Would the queen have reacted like *that*?" I gestured toward where Wren and Liam had disappeared. "Would she have screamed and puked when you ripped open her mind? Gods below, you could have *broken* that girl, Ulysses. For all we know, you did!"

Ulysses opened his mouth to argue, but I was done. "You heard Eden," I rolled over his words. "What if that's what it took? What if your idiocy—your sheer fucking *cruelty*—just let the queen back into this world?"

He faltered, his brow twitching down.

"You didn't think about that, did you?" I demanded.

"You just wanted to punish the queen so badly, you might have just *shattered* that girl and let the queen take her over!"

His mouth moved. "I... I didn't..."

I shook my head at him, my whole body quaking with fury. "I swear by all the gods, if you let that bitch back into this reality..."

Words failed me. Never in all my centuries had I wanted to hurt him this much.

And what was done, was done. If Ulysses broke her...

If Liam was alone with the queen now...

"Fuck!" I took off, racing after the direction I'd seen him heading. The manor was that way. I had to hope that was where he'd gone.

Unless she hurt him. Forced him to—

I shoved the thought down. Ulysses wasn't the only fool here. I shouldn't have stuck around yelling instead of chasing down Liam.

Every minute was too long, and by the time I reached the manor, a thousand nightmarish scenarios were already putting on stage productions inside my mind. I'd get back and find Liam dead. I'd find the whole house slaughtered. The manor would burn with him and the others trapped inside, and she'd be watching the flames, that same amused smile on her face that haunted my dreams.

I couldn't live with her in this world again. I couldn't witness those horrors a second time. Yet, if I killed the queen, the backlash would destroy me and half the countryside too. And even if I chose that suicide, the magic that bound me to the others would kill them as well, no matter where they were. That chain reaction was the cage we'd been caught in during all our time with her, unable to kill her for risk of killing each other and anyone nearby too.

But if she returned…

I slammed down into the front yard, shifting as I landed, and leapt up the steps to the entrance.

Barnaby had the door open before I could even reach the handle.

A breath of relief left me to see him. Not a line of his black suit was out of place; not a graying hair on his head had fallen astray. I knew the old demon could walk through a battlefield without gaining so much as a wrinkle to his attire, but even so, there was no hint on his face that the monster from our past had touched him. "Are they here?" I asked. "Liam and the girl?"

"Master Liam arrived several minutes ago, entering through the window of the southern guest room. He has since locked himself and his guest inside."

"What? Is he—"

"I hear nothing, Master Asher, except for a young lady crying." Unspoken was the question why, though I could see it in every proper line of his utter lack of expression.

I just didn't know how to answer him. "But is Liam okay?"

"Master Liam opened the door briefly to instruct us that they were not to be disturbed."

I hesitated. That was probably the most interaction Liam had given anyone outside of me, Ulysses, or Gideon for the better part of a century.

And it was for her sake?

Nodding distractedly to Barnaby, I continued inside,

feeling at a loss. There was a chance Liam had done that to protect everyone. Keep the others away from her, even if it meant being locked in a room with a nightmare. But possibly that wasn't the case at all. Possibly Wren hadn't broken, and the queen hadn't taken her over, and then...

If anyone understood pain, it was Liam.

I looked up the broad stairway leading to the higher floors. After what Ulysses had done to her, I had no idea how to face the girl. What shape she'd be in, or whether seeing me or anyone else would be too much, pushing her over the edge.

Gods below, I hoped Liam knew what he was doing.

Dragging my focus away from the stairs, I drew a breath and let it out slowly. There were still countless questions, ones whose answers would probably help her just as much as us. We needed to know who was behind the attack on the clinic, and why the rabids were suddenly so interested in turning and then recapturing a queen they'd murdered seven centuries ago.

I cast a short glance at Barnaby. "If you need me, I'll be in the north study. I need to make some phone calls."

## 15

WREN

*'m coming...*

Through hallways lined with corpses and cities engulfed in flames, I ran, but the laughing voice was always with me. Chasing me, taunting me in a cheery singsong that nonetheless surged at my back like a dark wave, ready to crash down and swallow me forever. And I couldn't escape it. Any moment now, it would descend, and I'd be lost.

Exhaustion dragged at my feet, slowing my steps, and unrelenting heat from the fires stole my breath. Every gasp took effort like I was lifting weights with my chest. Sweat stung my eyes, mingling with tears as sobs racked me because I couldn't keep running, couldn't go fast enough. I was going to die here, surrounded by those already dead. The wave would crush me down, burying me so deep that no one would ever know I—

Coolness spread through my mind like the gentle fall of snow. A new voice came, deep and kind, singing words I couldn't understand in a complex melody that stole my breath with its beauty. The fires faded and the dead did too, and there was only peace. Only the music spreading through the cool black world where nothing could harm me, and I would always be safe.

I opened my eyes.

Standing by the bed, Liam withdrew his hand from my forehead. I blinked up at him, the dreams melting away.

"That..." A breath left me. "I heard you."

A hint of a gentle smile crossed his face. He was beautiful, I realized. Now that he wasn't glaring at me with hate, he was breathtaking. Pale like a winter morning, like an ice sculpture, but without the coldness. His eyes were the color of a frozen lake, but not chilling. Merely secretive, hiding all kinds of untold treasure within their depths.

But to be lying here on the bed with him looking down at me, it wasn't just his beauty making it hard to breathe. With the terror of earlier gone and only the two of us here, something else in me began reacting to his presence. In tingles and warmth, my body started to wake, becoming hyperaware of the soft bed beneath me, the quiet of the room, and the hint of his scent on the air. Desire pooled in my middle like a swirling fire, stoked higher by the knowledge that, beneath the cotton blanket covering me, I was wearing only a thin hospital gown. The ease with which he could push it aside and touch all of me made my nipples harden and the flesh between my legs throb.

And the need didn't seem to be affecting only me. The

blue of his eyes darkened, heat entering his gaze. My bottom lip slipped between my teeth, and a breath pressed from him at the slight motion. What was this? First I was aroused by the mere sight of Asher, then I had a similar reaction to Ulysses. Now Liam?

God, I wanted him in the bed with me now. Everything in me craved it. I couldn't understand this fire inside of myself, this desire for these men, like some part of my *soul* was inside them, calling to me.

Even if that was insane.

Or another sign I was that monstrous queen.

Dragging my gaze from him, I tried to calm the arousal pounding through me, even while I couldn't decide how hard I'd keep that resistance up if he were to reach for me now. My need felt like a cliff, and all it would take was a touch of his hand to send me tumbling over the edge.

I'd only been with one other guy in my life. A prom date who'd barely been able to get it out of his jeans before he came. Fumbling around in the back seat of his Jeep hadn't been exactly thrilling, but this...

This was inexplicable. Incredible. My body yearned for Liam to be on top of me, in me, his hands all over me. The bloodied memories Ulysses had forced into my mind felt like a distant clamor. Surely they weren't responsible for the power of this need pulsing through me.

God, what was this? I was wet just lying here, every part of my body desperately ready for him. But that was madness. A short while ago, he and the rest wanted to kill me, for God's sake. I couldn't—

Struggle on his face, Liam took a step back, putting a

few feet of distance between himself and the side of the bed.

A shuddering breath entered my lungs, and I pushed away on the mattress, adding to the space between us. When I looked up at him, I could read the tension and maybe even a hint of apology in his expression. "How—" I cleared my throat. "How did you, um"—my hand made an aborted gesture to my head—"do that? How did Ulysses?"

He shrugged like it was hard to explain.

I hesitated. "Thank you."

A trace of a smile crossed his face, and I had to make myself keep breathing. God help me, he was beautiful.

Swiftly, he signed something.

"I-I'm sorry, I don't—"

"You're welcome." His voice was a harsh rasp, and I faltered, my arousal dying into cold pain. That vision. The one where he was covered in blood. The one where I'd known his voice was...was...

Oh my God.

Tears stung my eyes. How could anyone—how could *I* —have ever wanted to hurt this man?

Concern filled his expression. Lifting his hands in a small shrug, he gave me a questioning look I could easily read. *What?*

"It's just... I'm so sorry I—or whoever I was..." I struggled for words. "God, I'm so sorry for what I did to you."

His expression cleared into something so kind. He shook his head, mouthing the word "no." Glancing at the nightstand, he pulled open the drawer and took out a pad of paper and a pen, scribbling something on the small sheet.

*Not you.*

The letters were beautiful, like art unto themselves. I looked up at him as he signed something to me and then nodded to the note as if emphasizing what he'd just told me.

Worry gnawed at me. "How can you be sure?"

The kindness on his face deepened. He wrote something else swiftly. *Because you care.*

My brow furrowed. As metrics went, mere guilt didn't seem like it should count for much. Not against being the reborn soul of a torturing maniac who'd robbed him of his voice.

But set on a scale against how horrible Amalie had been, maybe possessing empathy was worth more than I thought.

"Why did... *she* do it?" I asked quietly.

He shook his head with an expression like it really wasn't important.

"Please."

Liam hesitated. His mouth tightened, and then he flipped the scrap of paper over. *She took what you loved, and I loved to sing.* He paused again. *And she grew bored of my screams.*

"My God..." On impulse, I moved over and reached out, taking his hand.

He tensed all over, freezing instantly like the ice sculpture I'd pictured him to be, and it was only too easy to see the conflict on his face.

Quickly, I released him. "Sorry."

Air entered his lungs. He shook his head dismissively.

I tucked my hand back beneath the blanket. I knew I'd

seen heat in his eyes earlier. It had been unmistakable. But that hadn't been heat just now.

That'd been something approaching fear.

I took a steadying breath, wondering if he just didn't like to be touched or if he wasn't as comfortable around me as he appeared. But then I didn't suppose it mattered. Either way, that was enough for me to know to keep my hands to myself for his sake.

Glancing around, I tried to focus on the room. I was still in the four-poster bed, silken curtains tied back on all sides and a cotton blanket covering me. Golden light spilled from the Tiffany lamps on the nightstands on either side of the bed and on the carved wood tables throughout the massive room, illuminating satin-covered furniture, though their light couldn't quite reach the distant ceiling. Beside the door at the far end, an enormous wardrobe of polished wood waited, big enough and antique-looking enough that I'd almost suspect it led to Narnia. Everything around me spoke of old-world elegance, from the darkened chandelier overhead to the arched windows to my left, the brocade curtains drawn over them tightly.

"What is this place?" I asked him.

The quickly written answer was simple. *Home.*

"Yours?"

He hesitated and then nodded, but I got the impression that wasn't the full answer.

"And is this...your room?"

*Guest room,* he wrote and then paused as if debating writing something else.

A knock came at the door before I could ask him about it, and I tensed.

Liam looked toward the sound, his eyes narrowing. Giving me a reassuring smile, he motioned for me to stay put and then headed for the door.

As he slipped outside, I drew the blanket around me. Sooner or later, I'd have to go out there.

I just couldn't imagine how I'd face anyone when I did.

## 16

### LIAM

"**I**s she okay?" Ulysses blurted the moment I stepped into the hall.

A black wall of rage roared up inside me, and I shoved him so hard, he crashed into the opposite side of the corridor.

He caught himself with one hand, holding the other out as if in entreaty. "Look—"

I slammed into him, punching him hard enough to snap his head sideways into the wall, denting the plaster.

He rolled to the side and then kicked me backward, summoning his knife when I immediately lunged at him again. "Liam, dammit—please!"

I stopped just short of the glistening blade, my fangs bared.

Eyes locked on me, Ulysses didn't breathe. "I'm not here to hurt her, man."

Fury rolled through me, making my body quake. With

a white-knuckled hand, I pointed away from the guest room, silently demanding he leave.

The fool didn't move. "Listen, I fucked up, all right? I did. But... I mean, is she still, you know, *her*? I didn't bring the queen back or—"

"Is that all you care about?" I snarled, my voice grating at my throat like a thousand tiny knives. How the hell he *dared* to come up here after what he did, I couldn't imagine. But that was Ulysses for you. Act first, question never, and damn the consequences.

But what he'd done to her...

I shuddered, fighting the urge to drive him through the wall into the next room—and possibly not stop there. Her screams had been horrible, her sobs gut-wrenching. Amalie never would have looked that shattered. That terrified. Wren's reaction had been visceral, and the way she'd cowered as if in fear one of us would hurt her more...

I'd lived that hell. That fear. That way you abased yourself in desperate hope the one hurting you would finally be sated, and the horrible way you retreated and cowered when they never were. And to see Wren reacting like that to us? To *me*?

My stomach churned. I never harmed an innocent. That was my promise to myself. No matter what I was capable of, the innocent would always be safe from me. But the cruel or the sadistic? Those who preyed upon anyone weaker than themselves, with no care for how their victims suffered? For them I had no mercy, and I'd see them bleed their way out of this life screaming, if I could.

Ulysses was my friend. Closer to me than what little family I'd ever known. On any other day, I'd never hurt him, and I'd kill anything that tried to cause him harm. But what he'd done to that innocent young woman...

That beautiful, *mesmerizing* young woman...

A ragged breath entered my lungs, inexplicable arousal clashing with my anger. After what happened with the queen, I'd never wanted to be with someone. The mere thought of anyone touching my body made a suffocating sort of anxiety instantaneously pour through my veins. And any kind of sexual contact?

Impossible.

Yet with Wren, I'd suddenly wanted everything. To feel her mouth on mine. To run my hands over her curves, her breasts, and every inch of her body until I made her moan with pleasure. I'd barely been able to resist the urge to tumble her in the sheets right then, thrusting myself into her until she screamed not from pain but exquisite ecstasy.

After seven hundred years of celibacy, the shift was... alarming.

I knew it changed nothing. My anxiety had paralyzed me when she so much as touched my hand, which meant there was no way I could do anything else. But for the first time in centuries, gods, I wished I could.

Though, of course, there was her own fear of us to consider.

*You terrorized her,* I signed at Ulysses.

He grimaced. "I know. I—"

*Stay away.* I pointed again.

Ulysses exhaled. "I will. I swear. I won't—"

*Now.*

He held up his hands. "I just need to know. Is she okay? Her, I mean. Not... not the queen. Just her. Please."

I eyed him. After so many centuries, I knew when the man was bullshitting, and right now...

He actually looked devastated.

*Hurting.* Irritation swelled in me. *No thanks to you.*

"Oh, Zeus, I'm sorry. I—"

"Apologize to *her*," I rasped.

Ulysses nodded fast and started for the door.

Alarmed, I blocked his path. *Later,* I signed emphatically.

He faltered, seeming lost in the middle of the hall.

I gritted my teeth. However bad he was feeling, I doubted it came close to the hell he'd poured into her mind. Projecting thoughts and illusions was a trick we used sparingly, to help and not to hurt.

He'd just violated the hell out of that—and her.

"Whatever she needs, I'll—" His voice was raw. "Just let me know."

My eyes narrowed, but he didn't even look at me, his gaze lingering on the room I wondered if Wren might eventually want to make her own. With a nod as if he was clinging to his own words, Ulysses turned and walked away.

# 17

## WREN

When Liam came back in, I had a suspicion who'd been outside, if only from the traces of anger on his face.

"Was that Ulysses?" I asked carefully.

He nodded. "You okay?"

"Yeah." My voice sounded strained to my own ears. "You?"

The corners of his lips rose. He nodded, and I tried for a smile in return, but it felt cracked. Liam was one thing. Kind, compassionate—shockingly so, considering what my past self had done to him. But Ulysses...

Shudders went through me. He clearly believed I was the same person who'd hurt him all those centuries ago, and even if the thought of what he'd suffered horrified me, that might not be proof for him like it was for Liam. The hate he had for me was chilling, and as for what else he might do to me now...

I shifted my shoulders as if to drive away the thought. I

couldn't hide in here forever, but that didn't mean I was ready to face *him.*

And God only knew what Asher or Gideon were thinking at this moment.

My eyes strayed to the window. Whatever it was they believed about me, on some level it couldn't be my main concern. I had no idea what time it was, but when last I'd seen my family, they'd been freaking out at the hospital because I'd been kidnapped by, well, vampires.

Not that they knew it.

God, they had to be worried sick.

"Do you, uh, think I could make a phone call?" I tried.

Liam hesitated. Holding up a finger in a gesture to wait, he went over to a small box on the wall that I hadn't noticed in all the opulence around me. Pressing a button on it briefly, he waited.

My brow drew down. What was that supposed to—

Another knock came, and a moment later, the door swung inward slightly. A woman with graying hair peeked her head around the corner, and she beamed a smile when she spotted me and Liam. "Hello, dears."

Liam signed to her, and she nodded, coming all the way into the room. A black dress covered her, the kind I imagined pioneers wore, and her gray hair was tied back in a bun. She appeared as if she could have stepped straight from the painting *American Gothic,* except for the way she never stopped smiling.

Quickly, Liam signed something else as she shut the door behind her.

"Oh," she agreed immediately. "Of course." She turned the smile on me. "We can certainly find you a safe phone to use. But I bet you'd like to get changed out of that dreadful hospital gown first, yes? Maybe a shower too?"

I looked from her to Liam and back, a wave of *yes, please* suddenly warring with my need to get in touch with my family.

But then, returning to them while still wearing a dirt-stained hospital gown with my hair a mess like I was a creature out of a horror movie? Yeah, that'd probably only make them more concerned. "Uh, sure. That'd be great."

Her smile broadened. "Mind clearing out for a bit?" she said to Liam.

He gave me a quick glance, as if checking that I was okay, and a flash of desire whipped through me again, offering up fantasies of asking him to join me.

A blush burned up my cheeks. I managed to give him a small smile before turning away, and a heartbeat later, I heard the door open.

"It's such a pleasure to meet you, dear," the woman said while he left. "I'm Frideswyd. You can call me Friday. The boys all do."

I blinked, realizing she meant the four guys I'd met. "Hi, I'm Wren."

"Oh, yes, I heard. We're so happy you're here."

I hesitated, not sure how that could be true. "We?"

"My husband, Barnaby, and I maintain the property." Friday walked to the wardrobe. "Now, let's get you cleaned up, shall we?"

She pulled the doors open and set to drawing out clothes.

I faltered. "Um, my size is—"

"Oh, don't worry. These will all fit you."

My brow rose. "But how did you..."

She chuckled, carrying over a shirt, jeans, even underwear and a bra. There was a pair of sneakers too, with socks tucked in them.

I stared at her.

"Perhaps a shower first?" She nodded to my left.

I glanced over and then froze. There was a carved wooden door standing slightly ajar just beyond the nightstand, and through the gap I could see a mirror reflecting a bathroom.

But I'd looked around the room earlier. That had just been a blank wall.

Ice spread through my veins. "What is this?"

Friday smiled. "We maintain the property, as I told you."

"What are you?" My heart raced. "What is this place?"

"*This* is our home, and I..." She seemed to consider how to respond, which only made my panic shoot higher. "Well, I'm your friend if you're mine."

"What does that mean?"

She sighed, still smiling, and set the clothes down on the edge of the bed before settling herself there as well. "You were turned recently, weren't you?"

I shifted position, uncomfortable at the question.

"And I'm guessing you didn't have much experience with the *unusual* before that, did you?" This time she didn't wait for me to answer. "This world is full of all kinds of marvelous things—some safe, some decidedly not. My husband and I fall into a middle category, the one that doesn't want to harm anyone but will protect those we've agreed to defend, which includes the boys and now includes you. We keep this house as a safe place for others, and for the past five hundred and thirty-seven years, it's been a home to the boys, as a thank-you for saving both our lives from some rather persistent exorcists."

I wasn't sure what to say. "Exorcists...?"

Amusement crossed her face. "Demons, dear. My husband and I are demons."

I stopped breathing.

Her brow rose pointedly, a smile still on her face. "We won't harm you, remember? Not unless you're a danger to us or our boys."

I hesitated, and she seemed to read into my silence.

"If you're thinking about the whole 'queen' thing, don't worry. You're still you. I can see that. There *is* something odd about you, but it's not her, and it's not a danger to us. The house never would have let you in here if it were. And as for the boys, well... you're not a threat to them." A teasing look came into her eyes. "*Quite* the opposite, actually."

My cheeks started to burn.

"Let's get you cleaned up, shall we?" She stood again, motioning to the bathroom.

I hesitated, but what other option was there? Stay here? Wander back home in a hospital gown, possibly terrifying my family more?

I climbed from the bed. Beyond the brand-new door, the bathroom was huge, featuring an enormous tub beside a glassed-in shower and a toilet tucked away in the corner. Two sinks waited below a mirror that took up an entire wall, and the row of bright lights inset in the ceiling made the ocean-blue tiles glisten. Fluffy towels hung from silver racks, and a luxurious white robe waited on a hook on the back of the door. The smell of lavender and vanilla filled the air, most likely coming from the soap bars by the sinks, while beside the shower, bottles of shampoos and conditioners waited, offering an array of choices.

Warily, I glanced back. "Y-you made this, didn't you? Somehow, you…" I gestured to the room, words failing me.

Friday smiled. "If you need anything, just use the buzzer on the wall there." She nodded to a small brass panel on the wall, a red button and mesh like a speaker on it. "I'll see you outside when you're done."

Without another word, she pulled the door closed behind her, leaving me alone in the impossible room.

***

I didn't think I'd taken a better shower in my life.

Sometime later, scrubbed and dressed with my hair dried by a blow dryer that looked like it had more settings than a TV remote, I made my way back to the bedroom door.

Liam was waiting when I opened it.

So was Friday.

I gave the woman my best attempt at a smile, though nervousness still tangled through me at the sight of her. A demon. Not just that. A demon who could make entire rooms appear like a magic trick and somehow knew my size.

Wonderland felt more stable than this house right now.

The place was beautiful, though. The hallway outside the bedroom was broad and stretched off to my right for a long way until ending in what looked like an opening for a staircase. Dark wooden doors lined the corridor on either side at distant intervals, like the spaces they hid were large too, and unlit sconces dotted the walls between them. To my left, another arched window stood, its thick satin curtains drawn tight. The ceiling was likewise dim, but there was a bizarrely *watchful* energy to it, even if all I could see was pale plaster and wood molding.

I returned my focus to the others, not wanting to look up there for long.

"This way." Friday started down the hall. "The house phone is downstairs."

Liam smiled at me. Together, we followed her, the thick runner carpet on the polished hardwood floor absorbing our steps entirely. All the doors along the hall were closed, and I couldn't hear anything from beyond the thick wood. At the end of the corridor, a broad staircase led down. I trailed the others as the steps carried us past two more floors before we finally reached the ground level.

It looked like a palace. Marble floors reflected the light of distant fixtures above us, and sconces along the walls illuminated paintings in rich colors and dark frames. Far ahead, I could see an arched pair of doors that seemed likely to lead outside, though without any daylight around them, I couldn't be sure.

"What *is* this place?" I murmured.

"Home," Friday said.

I glanced at the woman. "It's *huge*. Where are we?"

She gave a brief look to Liam as if checking it was okay to speak. The guy nodded. "About thirty miles outside the town where the boys found you."

I shook my head immediately. "No way. I definitely would have heard about a place like this."

Friday shrugged. "Well, we like to keep a low profile, at least on the outside. And the house protects itself." With a smile, she crossed the broad hall toward a door of carved wood. "This way, dear."

The door opened before she reached it. At the threshold, Gideon paused when he spotted us.

I couldn't read his expression. His face was entirely closed off, and when he spoke, his voice was so level I could have balanced on it. "Everything all right?"

Liam nodded while Friday smiled. "Perfectly fine," the woman said. "We were just on our way to the phone in the study."

For a moment, Gideon paused. "Right."

Something odd was in his voice, but he seemed to direct the tone to Friday and not me. Without another word, he turned and pushed the door open again.

I followed Friday and Liam when they walked into the room, my eyes not quite twitching up to Gideon's as I passed. He'd left space for us to enter, but doing so brought me close to him, and discomfort gripped me when I came near. He was bigger than the others, taller but broader too, like some warrior from the Scottish Highlands who probably should be swinging a sword to take off my head. I couldn't manage a full breath until I was past him into the study.

Only it was more like a library.

The room was expansive, easily fifty feet wide or more, with dark wood bookshelves built into all the walls, stretching up at least two stories high. A ladder on rollers was attached to the wall, and a gallery ran around the room above it. Windows that had to be at least twenty feet high lined one wall, but their curtains were drawn tight, no scrap of light getting through. Lamps filled the space, shining gold light across the study, reminiscent of the bedroom upstairs. To one side, a massive fireplace stood, so tall and wide I could probably walk straight into it. Two leather armchairs waited in front of it, small tables at their sides. On the other end of the room, a large oak desk sat, its top inset with red leather. A few books were stacked on it next to an antique phone with a brass receiver and a marble handle and base. The thing looked like the type of phone I'd seen in one of Harper's old cop dramas from the 1930s.

"Here you go, dear." Friday gestured to the device.

Biting my lip, I glanced between her and the guys, finding kindness on Liam's face and a look on Gideon's like I was a potentially deadly experiment that might explode.

But none of them were leaving the study, not even Friday.

So much for privacy.

I debated arguing, but to what end? The woman could make rooms appear out of thin air. Like the walls were going to stop her from listening in if she wanted?

And I got the impression Gideon wouldn't go, regardless.

Picking up the receiver, I spun the rotary dial. The call picked up on the second ring.

"Hello?"

A breath of relief pressed from my chest at the sound of my mother's voice. "Mom?"

"Oh." She chuckled. "Hi, Wren. What's up, honey?"

I paused, thrown. *What's up?* Last I'd seen her, she'd been red-faced and shouting at the nurses, terrified because I'd vanished out of a hospital room. "Um, I just wanted to check on you."

"Aw, you're so sweet."

Sweet? What? "A-are you okay, Mom?"

"Fine, honey."

Was someone listening to her? But then, she'd said my name. If she was trying to hide who was calling, she wouldn't have done that.

What the hell was going on?

I looked back at Friday, Liam, and Gideon. They were watching me, questions in their eyes. "Mom, is something wrong? You can tell me."

She laughed. "That's funny, sweetheart."

"Funny? Mom—" I didn't know what to do. "Is Dad there?"

"He's right here. Ted, it's Wren."

In the background, I heard my father respond, "That's nice. Hi, Wren."

He sounded like he was commenting on the weather.

My heart pounded. What was this? They sounded like themselves, but wrong—and not just because they weren't reacting like anyone whose child had gone missing for the second time only hours before. They sounded unfocused. Distracted. Like they were two steps shy of being high.

Mom and Dad's strongest "drug" was their morning coffee.

"Look," I tried. "Is Harper there? I'd really like to talk to her."

"Harper?"

A torrent of ice rushed through me. She sounded like she'd never heard the name.

"M-my sister, Mom."

"*Ohhh*, that's right." She laughed. "She's on a trip to Switzerland, dear. A college thing."

"College... Mom, Harper never said a word to me about going to Switzerland. She doesn't even have a passport."

Mom was quiet. "Huh, that is funny." She chuckled like she was baffled. "So where are you, dear?"

Every instinct I had suddenly clamored for me not to say a single word about this place. "Where's Harper?"

"Harper?"

Same tone. Like I was reminding her my sister existed. "*Harper!* Your daughter! Mom—"

"Where are you, Wren?"

"What's wrong with you? Where's—"

"Wren, where are you?" Her pleasant tone sounded like a cracking veneer, and I suddenly didn't want to know what was on the other side. "Wren?"

"I, um—"

"Where are you, Wren?"

"Mom—"

"Wren." My father's voice joined in from the background. "Where are you?"

"Yes," my mother continued. "Where are you, Wren?"

"Where are you, Wren?" my father asked on top of her words.

"Where are you?"

"Where are you?"

They didn't stop, both of them speaking at the same time like a pair of cuckoo clocks going off simultaneously. "Where are you, Wren? Where are you? Where are you, Wren—"

I slammed the phone down and retreated, staring at the thing like it might bite me.

"What happened?" Gideon asked.

I jumped. Trembling all over, I looked at them. "Did you do that?" I demanded of Friday.

The woman appeared confused. "I simply provided a phone, dear."

I couldn't decide whether to trust the words. Somewhere along the line, I'd passed so far beyond my depth that now I felt like I was treading water in the middle of the ocean, and God knew what sharks swam below.

Gideon took a step toward me, and my attention snapped to him. "What happened?" he asked again, his words careful.

My head shook. "Harper's gone. My twin sister. And they don't care. They barely even seem to *remember* her. They just kept asking where I was."

He glanced at Liam, who signed something quickly to him and Friday. The woman nodded and hurried from the room.

"What?" I asked. "What was that?"

"We'll look into a few things," Gideon replied.

I hesitated. That wasn't what Liam said. I didn't know sign language—something I'd damn well start fixing if I spent too much longer here—but I could still read the look on his face. "Do you know what this is?"

Gideon made a hedging noise. "We need to check a—"

"Don't patronize me. Do you know?"

He hesitated. "Not yet. But we will."

A breath left me. "I want to go back to my house."

At my words, Liam gave me an alarmed look.

"It's still daylight," Gideon said.

I turned away. That only mattered if I bought into this vampire thing, and I still wasn't sure I did. These guys being *something*? Sure. Friday being a demon? Okay, well, the house was proof she wasn't human, anyway. I could accept nonhumans existed, and maybe even that I was some kind of reincarnated monster, mostly because I had no choice.

But that didn't mean anything about me being a *vampire*.

And even then... "I thought you said Ulysses and Asher left, though."

He hesitated. "It's complicated."

Of course it was. "Well, if they can go out, then I don't see why I can't—"

"We're not like you."

"What the hell is that supposed to mean?"

"What I said."

My God, the man was a brick wall. Shaking my head, I turned away. "Is the phone still safe?"

He paused. "It should be."

His voice sounded cagey, but I didn't care. With a quick nod, I picked up the receiver again. Before I argued to go outside, daylight be damned, I needed more information.

And, hopefully, I knew just who to call to get it.

## 18

---

ULYSSES

I had to make this up to Wren.

Even if I couldn't *begin* to imagine what would ever be enough.

I gunned the engine of my motorcycle, flying down the old state road. Liam said I should apologize, and the gods knew he was right, but the gods also knew apologies alone would never be sufficient. Not for what I'd done.

I'd never felt such shame in all my life.

I drove faster. Asher and the rest were right. I'd been a bastard beyond description for what I did to Wren. My fear of Amalie blinded me, making me see only the monster from my past.

And not the innocent young woman she was tormenting.

Bile burned at the back of my throat. That was the truth, wasn't it? I'd seen the fear on Wren's face when Amalie tried to exert her presence. The way Wren cowered on the hospital bed after beating back the ghost of Amalie's power. She was as much a victim of Amalie as the rest of us, only she had to contend with that monster actually still *living* inside her mind. It was a sheer miracle what I'd done hadn't given Amalie all the foothold she needed to kill Wren entirely.

And who was to say how long Wren could hold out, anyway?

No, apologies would never be enough. She needed answers and help and anything I could give her. Asher was already making calls; I'd heard that much on my way out the door. But some of the best sources rarely answered the phone, which meant I could do more good out here than anything.

I didn't care if I had to drive to Alaska or take a plane to China. I'd help her somehow.

Only then—maybe—could I ask Wren for forgiveness.

I veered off the old state road and into the lot outside the Kicked Bucket Bar, my tires flinging gravel and dust as I skidded to a halt. The building ahead of me was a wreck —one ramshackle story of rotted wood siding around grimy windows with bars over the front and neon signs glowing past the filthy glass. At this time of day, a handful of vehicles sat in the lot, and Laz's red pickup was the only one I recognized.

But then he was the guy I'd come to see anyway.

Jumping the two steps up to the porch, I yanked off my gloves and helmet, shoving the former into the latter and then skimming my gaze over the lot and the road beyond. In broad daylight, rabids wouldn't be out, not unless they wanted to burn instantly to ash. Only the Sentinels could withstand the sun, though that still left about a million things that could be a problem out here, not the least of which were those damn GSS bastards who probably were still hunting Wren.

And the Kicked Bucket welcomed them all—albeit grudgingly where the government was concerned.

Tugging open the door, I ignored the sticky residue the handle left on my fingers and continued inside. Barely any sunlight made it past the filthy windows, though a few random overhead bulbs tried valiantly to beat back the shadows. An array of tables and seats were to my left, and only one in the back was occupied.

I paused, a sense of wrongness coming from the man that made no sense. The guy was a rabid, but... here? With daylight outside? Sure, he was safe in the dark interior of the bar, but how the hell had he gotten into this place to begin with?

Keeping an eye on him, I headed farther inside. The bar itself stretched away along the right-hand wall, while the bartender stood behind it, wiping down the counter and watching me as I came in.

"Hey, Laz," I said.

The man nodded in wordless greeting. At first glance, Lazarus didn't look like much. His body was short and stocky, his hair an indeterminate shade of grayish brown. His olive skin wasn't young but wasn't overly wrinkled either, placing him at any age from thirty to sixty, while his plaid shirt and jeans were more function than fashion.

He also spoke more languages than even Gideon knew, and he had managed bars from here to outer

Mongolia over the course of a couple millennia. Not a thing on earth would kill him, from guns to nuclear bombs.

We'd been friends for nearly six hundred years.

"Wondering if you could help me with a question," I continued, watching the only other occupant of the bar from the corner of my eye. "A group of unfriendlies attacked a girl a few nights back. You heard anything?"

"Hmm. Don't think I can help you."

I paused. I knew that tone. Laz thought this guy was trouble too, then. Good to know.

"All right, fair enough." I leaned against the counter. "What's on tap?"

Laz's lip twitched. "Whatever the hell I want to serve."

I chuckled, but I could read the tension in his body. "Sounds terrible."

"Probably should just head on, then." He placed four fingers on the bar.

My eyebrow rose. Four guys, not just the one.

But right now, I welcomed a fight—especially one that might give me answers that could help Wren. "Eh, it's too bright out there. Think I'll hang out a while."

"Suit yourself." Laz returned to wiping the counter.

I walked toward the guy at the table.

His back to me, the man didn't turn around, but his stench reached me before I made it another ten feet. Definitely a rabid. Old one, too. I circled wide, watching him as I moved.

He didn't look away from his drink.

"Hey, maybe you can answer my question." I eyed the rear hallway of the bar before returning my attention to the man at the table. The others would be down there, I was fairly certain. No windows. Plenty of shelter from sunlight. But for the moment, they weren't a concern. "You wouldn't happen to know about a handful of dead rabids, would you?"

The guy's gaze crept up to me. His eyes were blood-shot, and the white of one of them was entirely stained red. He wasn't doing well, which only brought back the question of what the hell he was doing *here.* Someone in his condition should have been devouring anything in sight, not sitting quietly in a bar.

"You mean the ones you killed, Sentinel?" His voice was rough, like his vocal cords had started to decay, and his lips pulled back in a grin, revealing rotted fangs and flecks of gristle clinging between his teeth.

Lovely.

"Why are you so interested in the girl?"

He chuckled. "What *girl*?"

I studied him. The way he said the word was odd, as if "girl" was a joke somehow. "The one your friends turned before I made them ash. The one *more* of your friends took on the entire North City Clinic trying to capture... except they failed. Come to think of it, your kind seem to be failing quite a bit lately."

Rage flashed through the man's eyes. "You have no *idea* what you're dealing with."

"Then why don't you enlighten me?"

The man chuckled, cold rage in the sound. "Nah. I think I'll just kill you instead."

Behind my back, a door opened. I retreated a step, keeping the rabid in view while I glanced at the hall.

Three more rabids walked from the storage room.

"This it?" I asked dryly.

The first guy's lips curled back in a snarl. "You really want to do this? All alone?"

My knife materialized in my hand, and I smiled. "Definitely."

The man lunged for me, but I was already moving, darting to the side and slashing at him as he passed. He scrambled out of the way, dodging the knife, though my blade still nicked his arm. Howling, he fell back, not dead yet though the blade's touch would eat into him. But then the other three were coming for me, shoving past one another with their hands out like claws and their fangs bared.

Sloppy idiots.

Before the nearest one made it two steps, I slashed my blade through his throat, turning him to ash. Another grabbed for my wrist, trying to dislodge my weapon. Twisting in his grip, I shifted to shadow for only a heartbeat, letting the knife fall and then snagging it again before it hit the ground. Slicing upward, I tore the metal through him and then spun as he crumbled.

The third rabid slammed into me from the side, shrieking as he clawed at my throat. I crashed into a table, but the momentum shifted his balance to my advantage. Shoving him hard, I propelled him past me and through the air. Laz swore as glasses and bottles shattered when the rabid collided with the wall behind the bar, but I didn't pause. Rolling back to my feet, I hurled the knife through the air and impaled him.

And then there was one.

I looked back to the first guy while my knife vanished from the pile of ash by the bar that had been a rabid only a moment before. "So. About that girl."

The man shook his head. "He'll kill me."

My eyes narrowed. "Who?"

"It doesn't matter what you do to me. He'll do worse." A crazed light showed in the rabid's eyes. "He's the end and the beginning. He is all."

The rabids were joining cults now. Awesome.

I nodded slowly. "Right..." I took a step closer to him. "But you know what he isn't? *Here*. And I am. So tell me. What do you want with the girl?"

"We need her. You don't understand what she is."

"The queen."

He laughed like I was a fool. "The *queen*? You think *that's* all this is about? She's the key, Sentinel. The key to everything, and he won't stop. Not until he has her. He's already got the other one. He'll do whatever it takes to... to..."

"What other one?" I demanded.

The rabid didn't answer. Shaking his head, he staggered backward, his face twitching and confusion filling his eyes. "No. No, please, I didn't. I swear, I wouldn't—"

A scream tore from him, the sound agonized. He convulsed as suddenly flames chewed their way out of his chest. Howling as the fire engulfed him, he thrashed, falling back onto a table and then crumbling to dust.

What the hell?

I glanced around quickly, but there was no one else here. Just me and Laz, and I trusted him not to do something like this. And distance didn't necessarily mean anything anyway, not where curses were concerned.

Except I hadn't seen anything like that in centuries. Seven of them, in point of fact. The only thing close to it was the night Amalie died, when everyone around her died too—except us.

Fuck.

I looked back at Laz. His face was somber, but a dry expression flickered through his eyes when he met mine.

"You just *had* to aim for the liquor shelf, didn't you?"

"Sorry."

He scoffed. "I'll send you the bill." His eyes returned to the smoking pile of ash, the humor fading.

"How long have they been here?" I asked.

"Since just before sunrise. Bought drinks and told me they were waiting."

"They say what for?"

"Given this? I'm guessing *you*."

That was what I was afraid of. Except it didn't make any sense. Rabids didn't seek us out. They hid.

And yet these four had camped out as if knowing one or more of us would come here eventually.

I scanned the destruction. This was bad, but it was also insane. What the hell had they thought they'd gain by fighting me here? A distraction?

A delay?

*He's already got the other one...*

Chills crept through me. I needed to get back to the manor *now*.

Turning, I wove through the remaining tables,

heading for the exit. "Laz, you, uh... you watch out for yourself, eh?"

"You know what this is about?" he called.

Pausing at the door, I glanced back at the pile of ash and the tendrils of smoke still drifting into the air. "Nothing good."

**19**

———————

WREN

I hung up the phone. Brayden didn't know where Harper was. Neither did Ollie nor Emma. I'd even asked Friday for a laptop and checked every social media account my sister possessed. But there was nothing. No indication she was at college or with friends or even that she'd lost her mind and gone on some kind of international rampage.

My sister had vanished, and Mom and Dad didn't even seem to realize it.

Or care.

I looked back at the rest of the study. Liam was gone—something about getting us food—and only Gideon remained. Somewhere in the past *however* many minutes it had been since I started calling everyone I could think of, he'd taken up residence in one of the chairs by the fireplace, a book lying open on his lap—not that I'd gotten the impression he was reading a word of it. The man just kept watching me, his face imitating a wall and his answers damn near monosyllabic.

"Nothing?" he asked neutrally.

I shrugged, unsure whether to scream or cry. "Nobody's heard from her. But... Harper wouldn't just leave the country. That's crazy. That..." I ran out of words to cover the sheer madness of that proposition.

Gideon nodded. "Ah." He set the book aside. "In that case—"

Footsteps came from beyond the study, and a moment later the door opened. Ulysses strode into the room, only to freeze when he saw me.

My stomach twisted. I wanted to retreat, but there was nowhere to go, and memories blurred through my mind at the sight of him. All I'd done in my former life. Every horror he'd unleashed in my mind and all the agony I'd caused him. Ulysses faltered, his mouth opening as if to say something to me, and then a pained look flashed over his face, like seeing me upset him.

Fair enough.

I turned away, wishing I could melt through the floor.

"Did you need something?" Gideon asked, his voice cold.

"Um..." Ulysses cleared his throat. "Yeah, uh... Gideon, can I speak to you for a second?"

A creak of leather came from the chair as Gideon rose to his feet. Without a word, he followed Ulysses from the room.

The low murmur of their voices carried from the hallway, their words unintelligible, and other voices joined a moment later.

I rubbed my upper arms, trying to shake the chill of the memories.

"Wren?" Gideon came back into the room. Ulysses trailed him with Asher and Liam behind. Liam set a small plate aside the moment he entered the room, the strange white cube-like substance atop it utterly ignored.

But at the looks on their faces, dread crept over me. "What is it? What's wrong?"

Gideon bobbed his head toward Ulysses, who hesitated. Liam signed something at him, sharp and emphatic. With a wince, he nodded.

"I, uh... I hear you have a twin sister," Ulysses started.

Oh, God. "What happened? What do you—"

"I don't know anything for sure."

I waited, my racing heart feeling weak, as if it couldn't pound hard enough for the panic surging through my veins.

He grimaced. "I had a run-in with a few rabids—"

"*Rabids?* Oh my God, did those things take her?"

The ground felt unsteady. I wanted to run from the feeling, if only to find her faster.

"I don't know," Ulysses said. "But one of them—" He glanced back at the others, clearly reluctant. "He admitted they wanted to capture you, but he also said they already have 'the other one.'"

My blood went cold. "Harper."

He made a hedging motion. "I'm not *sure* they meant—"

"No, they've got Harper." I shook my head, not a doubt in my mind. "She... Harper wouldn't vanish, and my parents are acting weird, and...” I started for the door. “I have to find her.”

Asher moved to intercept me immediately. “It’s not safe—”

“I don’t care. If these things have her—”

“The sun is still up,” Gideon interjected.

“So what?”

They stared at me.

I scoffed. “I’m not a vampire, okay? And even if you think I am, you all went outside. So why can’t I—”

“It’s not the same,” Gideon persisted.

“How?”

He glanced at the others.

Asher grimaced. “It’s complicated.”

“*How?* If you guys can go out, then I don’t see why I can’t—”

“If she is truly the queen reborn—” Gideon interrupted, addressing the others. “—and the bond is still there, there is a possibility that we could—”

“No!” Liam cut in, his rasping tone furious.

Ulysses shook his head hard. “We can’t risk it, man.”

“A possibility you could do what?” I demanded.

“It doesn’t matter,” Asher said. “Even if you could, these are still rabids. Taking you into a fight is foolish.”

“This is my sister we’re talking about. You’re not trapping me here!”

Liam made an angry sound. “Sunlight could *kill* you!”

I tried not to groan out loud.

Bobbing his head slightly, Gideon amended, “Or it might not.”

Liam threw his hands in the air like he couldn't believe them.

God, they really bought into this whole vampire thing about me, didn't they?

"It would be good to know," Asher allowed. "Not necessarily for this, but in general."

Liam signed something furiously.

"Exactly," Ulysses snapped. "Your little experiment could end up with her dead."

Gideon frowned. "It could work, though."

"*What* could?" I demanded. At their silence, I persisted. "Listen, you guys need to explain exactly what the hell you're talking about, *right* now. I'm standing right here, and you can't keep talking over me. Either let me show you I can handle sunlight or get out of my way."

The four of them regarded me, worried and curious and guarded by turns.

"Very well," Asher said. He nodded toward the window.

Liam instantly made a protesting noise.

"What the hell?" Ulysses cried.

"She wants to try, so I say we let her try. Wren?" Asher motioned for me to come with him.

I started across the room, only to have Liam grab my arm and pull me back, a frantic look on his face. With one hand, he signed swiftly to the others, and I couldn't hope to understand what he was saying.

But Asher looked away.

"You want to be the one to lead with that then?" Gideon asked.

Liam tensed, looking offended.

"He's right," Ulysses said. "We should deal with the other stuff first. Just in case."

"If this is enough," Asher said, "then that part won't be needed."

"What part?" I asked.

"Nothing," Asher directed the statement almost entirely to Liam and Ulysses.

"Bullshit," I retorted.

Respect glinted in Liam's eyes, along with satisfaction.

"Then *I* will explain," Gideon said firmly, as if irritated with them all.

I waited, eyeing the man warily.

"There are certain things you should know about us," Gideon continued to me. "And about you."

## 20

WREN

I stared as Gideon motioned for the men to go, alarm spreading through me. "What's that supposed to mean?"

Asher nodded to the others, and Liam grimaced. Ulysses hesitated, appearing on the verge of saying something to me, though God only knew what that would be.

But then he just scrubbed a hand over his hair and followed the others out the door.

My eyes slid back to Gideon. What the hell did he need to be alone to discuss? And why *him*? I mean, sure, he didn't look like he wanted to kill me anymore. Hadn't looked like that, really, since we were at Eden's place.

No, ever since Eden's, he'd just gone back to looking at me like I was a creature he'd happily dissect, but only if he could do so with a ten-foot pole, possibly while wearing a hazmat suit.

As the door closed, Gideon nodded for me to join him by the fireplace. Warily, I followed him over and lowered myself into the leather wingback chair opposite his own. His expression was solemn, and a pit formed in my stomach at the sight.

"What is it?" I asked.

For a long moment, he said nothing, as if collecting his thoughts. I watched him. His mouth was a grim line amid his red beard. Despite his build like a towering weightlifter and his eye patch like a pirate, he had the air of a stern professor, one with an unpleasant task before him.

He drew a breath. "There is a reason we are unaffected by sunlight unlike any other vampire."

I didn't move a muscle.

"The witch told you we were tied to you. This... *may* be true."

My brow twitched down. "I thought, based on what Eden said—"

"We may only be tied to the queen *in* you, in which case *you* are nothing to us at all."

I blinked, taken aback at the blunt statement. Admittedly, I didn't really know these men. Well, beyond those horrible memories, anyway. In reality, we'd only met a day or so ago. But the coldness in his voice... the distance...

Like I was an insect to him, maybe, or a passing puff of cloud. Here and gone. Meaningless.

And it hurt. It really did, even if he was barely more than a stranger. I couldn't deny that I was attracted to him, despite the fact he was clearly a jerk. He was hot in a pirate meets mountain man meets weightlifter sort of way, and having this sexy man be so *obviously* contemptuous of me...

I couldn't help it. It stung.

"But as much as the four of us were tied to Amalie," he continued in the same detached tone. "The Sentinels are also tied to one another. If one of us dies, the others are weakened or possibly killed as well. But our servitude also came with certain... perks. We are a unit, bonded to one another through magic, blood, and suffering. Even when we are apart, we are still connected, able to feel each other's pain. Able to know if the others are safe or harmed. And when we are together, we share everything. Living space. Trust. Even, at times,"—his eyes flicked over me—"women."

I swallowed hard. They...

Suddenly, I didn't know where to look in the room. Not at him, that was for damn sure. The guy thought I was nothing to them. But my memories from when I first laid eyes on him at the hospital flashed through my mind. How I'd seen a vision of them all having sex with me, and how it was to be with multiple men at once. After the hell the queen put them through, some part of me was surprised they'd ever wanted to do that again.

The rest of me was blushing hot at the realization I kind of wished I could experience that for real.

Except, of course, with the way Gideon thought I was *nothing,* Ulysses basically hated me, and Liam didn't like to be touched, that wasn't ever going to be an option.

I cleared my throat, but my voice still felt hoarse when I spoke. "So, what does this have to do with the sun?"

"Because we also share... gifts." His lecturing tone persisted, and he seemed to be ignoring the way my face was probably as bright as a stoplight. "Not the least of which is the ability to resist the sun. Alone of all other vampires, we can go out in daylight and not die, and—as long as she was bonded to us as well—the queen could too."

My attention darted to the covered windows.

"But," he continued pointedly, "you are not her. Not entirely. So there is only a chance that it would work for you." He studied me with utter disdain. "Especially as you are now."

"What..." My voice felt breathless. "What does that mean?"

He leaned back in the chair, radiating the patience of a professor lecturing a slow student. "You are a newly made vampire. You've never fed from anyone nor changed shape. And you are... inexperienced with us in other regards." Again, his eyes flicked over me, and I could read the innuendo there.

God, my face felt like it was on fire.

He didn't react to the fact. "Thus, the bond that existed between the queen and the four of us is, at best, weak inside you. Most likely it doesn't exist at all outside Amalie's presence in you, regardless of what Eden said. Whatever you *think* you feel, it may be nothing more than a passenger attached to your soul, same as the queen herself. It is not *you*. Therefore, it is possible the magic that enables us to resist the sunlight has not carried over to you, and that, if you were to go outside right now, you would die."

I wasn't sure what to say. How to feel. His tone was insulting as hell and made me want to defend myself on pure principle. I felt *something* when I was around them, after all. I'd assumed it was that bond. How could he be so sure it wasn't?

And, hell, that was even assuming I believed him. That I believed I was a *vampire*.

These hot guys were messing with my head.

"Yet," he persisted, "seeing as how there is no way to pass that magic on to you—"

"What?"

His mouth tightened as if annoyed at my interruption. "One person cannot take it on alone. The magic diffuses the impact of sunlight amongst all of us to the degree that the resulting pain is negligible. On one person alone, it won't work."

"But—" God, I couldn't believe I was arguing this with him. "You said the queen—"

"The queen didn't put the magic on herself. She only subjected us to it and then reaped the benefits of our connection to her. The spell itself was excruciating, and it died with her. Even if we could cast that magic on you now, the pain would incapacitate you for days while you felt as if you were being burned alive—assuming you even survived it."

I stared at him. "But if you're all tied together, then you could feel it. When she... with the spell, and then... I mean..." I couldn't say the words for what I knew she'd done to them. "When she hurt each of you. You all felt that, didn't you?"

He nodded tightly, a hint of a haunted expression breaking past his detached exterior. "Yes."

I wanted to throw up.

"The bond was quite ingenious of her. A brutal way to

extend the pain she loved to inflict. And it did not stop with that alone. The bond ensured none of us sought to escape her captivity through suicide, as we would be condemning our fellow Sentinels to death as well."

I hesitated. "You sound like you resent it. That connection, I mean."

He looked back up, his one eye locking on me. "I resent many things"—his voice was firm —"but not these men."

My insides quivered at the iron in his gaze. "I'm so sorry."

The coolness returned to his expression, and he looked away. "A kind gesture, but pointless. What's done is done. You claim you are not Amalie. Thus, you cannot apologize for her."

I fought the urge to fidget on the chair.

"However," Gideon continued. "As long as a trace of the bond is in you, there is a chance the protection from the sun would extend to you as well. That is what Asher wished to test, and what Liam and Ulysses are opposed to doing."

"And you?"

He inclined his head slightly. "I am never opposed to experiments if they are needed, but I prefer optimal conditions for success."

"What's that mean?"

"That you are weak."

A breath left me. "God, you just come right out and say what you're thinking, don't you?" I couldn't keep the anger from my voice.

He met my eyes with a pointed look. "You haven't fed.

Not but the once when you first woke after your death, and that is scarcely enough to sustain even the strongest of vampires for very long."

Shifting position in the chair, I looked away.

"You *are* a vampire, Wren. Or has it escaped your notice that you haven't eaten anything for nearly two days?"

I faltered. "I-I've just been nervous. And it's not like it's been the best couple of days I—"

"You need to feed from us."

"*What?*" I shot out of the chair.

"Not always," he allowed. "Not every day. But you will. If part of that bond exists in you, then we are safe for you to use in this fashion. You—"

"I'm not *using you,* Gideon!"

He regarded me like my little bug self had just done an odd trick.

A hoarse scoff escaped me, and I backed away, my eyes darting around and my heart pounding. I wanted out of here. This was a madhouse. Here was a man who *clearly* felt nothing but contempt for me, and yet he insisted I was a vampire who should drink his blood like... what? A milkshake?

My gorge rose.

"It will not hurt me, Wren." He pushed to his feet, taking a step toward me even as I retreated. "Feeding is... intense, but typically pleasurable for all concerned, at least when it's done willingly. But feeding from humans carries risks to them, and demons carry risks to you. Your options are limited. This will sustain you, and perhaps strengthen you enough that, should we test whether the bond has given you resistance to sunlight, you would survive."

He began rolling up his sleeve.

My eyes went wide. "No! No way. I'm not—"

"It is this or wait until nightfall. As you are not inclined toward that option, this is what is left to us."

I bumped into the door. He was still coming toward me, his sleeve now rolled above his elbow and his face...

"Gideon, d-do you even *want* me to...?"

His expression closed down. Hard. "That is not the important thing."

I recoiled. "Hell, *yes,* that's the important thing! Oh my *God,* what do you take me for?" I fumbled for the handle. "This... this is sick. I'm not a vampire, and you're just..." I held out a hand like I stood a chance of keeping him back. "You stay away from me."

Yanking open the door, I fled the room.

**21**

---

GIDEON

That had not gone like I anticipated.

I hesitated before rolling my sleeve back down. To be sure, I'd felt conflicted at the prospect of Wren feeding from me. The experience was… intense. Erotic. I would not be able to control my attraction to her once it began, nor keep her at the distance I needed for my own safety. To protect the others, I had been willing to allow it. After all, Asher was clearly torn. He seemed to *want* her to be part of us, and thus was permitting himself to be tempted too easily. Ulysses' mental state was unknown, and allowing him alone with her to potentially assault her mind again could jeopardize us all. And Liam didn't deserve the torment her touch would bring him.

But the risks filled me with nausea all the same.

Wren was not the queen. On countless levels, I could tell Wren was not the queen. She was a beautiful woman who filled my head with fantasies I simply would *not* entertain. Not when she had a trace of Amalie in her. Not when I couldn't be sure how much of what I saw was Wren and how much might be Amalie playing mind games.

The mere thought of that creature coming near me again was enough to send spikes of terror through me like I was a child.

My single eye was all I had left. For centuries, it had been my only hope of exploring my dearly loved world of books. Amalie took the other and would have taken both had I not agreed to be bound to her. She'd chosen me for unknown reasons, arriving at my monastery one day and caring nothing for my dreams as a scholar, and when I said no...

I shuddered. I'd learned to give her what she wanted in the years that followed. Pain and suffering were the trade for continuing to be able to read the great works of the world. But every moment had been filled with a dread that gnawed away at me, becoming my ever-present companion as time dragged on. Amalie's favor was mercurial, and she never failed to remind me how easily she could rob me of what I loved most, just as she had for Liam and the others.

Yet, despite the risk some trace of that monster might resurface, I was still drawn to Wren. Her mere presence was enough to plague my mind with erotic fantasies of using every trick I'd ever learned from a book and exploring each position I'd experienced over the centuries. And every passing minute worsened the draw. My treacherous body yearned for her, thrumming with the desire to take her on the desk, before the fireplace, against the bookcases...

In my bed...

I buttoned my cuff into place and then smoothed my shirt sleeve, willing my pulse to slow. The revulsion on Wren's face at my offer of a vein had been... unexpected. If she were anything like Amalie, the prospect of feeding from her "property" should have excited her. But no matter how closely I watched for even a trace of eagerness, I found nothing.

Less than nothing. I may as well have offered her the rotted carcass of a dead dog.

But I shouldn't trust it. Shouldn't feel guilt at how I'd behaved either, which made the sour twisting in my stomach absurd, to say the least. Logically, the girl was most likely a trap, albeit a complicated one, and eventually, it would be sprung—whether by her or someone else. Thus, keeping her at the farthest distance I could manage while still assuring all our safety was the only option. If she disliked me—and the gods knew I'd given her enough reason with my deliberately callous words—so much the better. Yes, I'd probably hurt her. Yes, that had been my plan. And yes, irrationally, I felt like an ass for it. But my behavior would help us both keep any interactions strictly to a minimum. That was for the best, for all our sakes. And once we determined how to rid her of this trace of Amalie, Wren could go on her way.

My chest ached at the thought.

Clearing my throat to assuage the feeling, I focused my attention on reclaiming my book from the end table. Valcher's *Treatise on Comparative Agriculture in Eighteenth-*

*Century Western Europe.* It was seventy-sixth on my current list of books to read, and the first thing I'd been able to grab while Wren used the phone Friday had provided via magic.

I wove past the chair on my way to the bookshelf, only for my steps to falter when I caught a hint of Wren's intoxicating scent still hanging on the air. Warm vanilla laced with rosewater, perhaps from the soap of her shower. A trace of cinnamon was there too, along with a twist that was unique to her and arousing beyond belief.

Exhaling sharply, I made myself keep moving and placed the book back into its slot on the shelf. While she was making her call earlier, it had been difficult to concentrate on reading. Listening to the intonation of her voice and trying to interpret how much of her personality was *her* and how much was Amalie took up most of my attention.

As had the distraction of my own fantasies.

I pressed a hand to the leather spines. As always, the comforting stability and infinite possibility of the books calmed me.

The study door swung open. It wasn't Wren, as some part of me expected, but instead, Ulysses.

"I take it that went well," he said dryly.

Indignation stirred in me. "Indeed. It appears you are not the only one making an almighty botch of this."

He looked away. I returned my attention to the books, irritated as much by my own slip of emotion as I was by him. What would I have preferred? That I let the girl feed on me?

My cock ached with desire. I exhaled forcefully,

ordering myself to calm down. "Is there something you required?"

Ulysses was silent, and I didn't look his way. If he was smart, he'd leave. There wasn't anything further to discuss.

And this was distracting. It was *all* distracting, from her scent on the air to the way my body craved her, to say nothing of the questions about her still hanging unspoken around me.

I should return to my room and take a cold shower, if only to regain focus.

"You think she could withstand the sun?" Ulysses asked quietly.

I scoffed. "I think experiments should be undertaken with care, and throughout this whole exercise, most of you have exhibited anything *but*."

"Man, I know I fucked up. But—"

"*Do* you?" I looked at him sharply. "Because now she is *here*, staying in the manor like a guest who has nowhere else to go, and there are no guarantees her purported innocence is not merely Amalie playing games with us all!"

Ulysses was quiet for a moment. "You really believe that?"

I ground my teeth. "I don't know what to believe."

Returning my attention to the books on the shelf, I skimmed the titles. Among these tomes, there would surely be an answer to this situation—one that didn't involve getting any closer to Wren than absolutely necessary. "We only need her around long enough to deal with this bit of the queen, and then she can leave."

From the corner of my eye, I saw Ulysses look away, his face tightening.

"It's for the best," I insisted. "The girl is nothing to us. A vessel for Amalie at most. Nothing more. We needn't let her be a distraction."

"*That's* what you're calling the way this feels?"

I pressed a hand to the leather book spines. "And if it is only the queen inside her eliciting that from us? Using her magic on us as she did all those centuries ago?"

Ulysses was silent.

"We've all carved out a space of peace here. It would be foolish to jeopardize that now." I drew a book down from the shelf and gripped it tightly. "Just in case we're wrong."

## 22

### WREN

Half an hour ago, this place had been Wonderland.

Now it felt like a cage.

I strode out of the study and down the long hall toward the double doors I'd thought earlier might lead outside. I wasn't what the Sentinels said. I wouldn't be. And if Gideon and the rest didn't want to let me prove that by exposing me to something as simple as goddamn *sunlight*, that didn't mean I had to believe them.

Gideon's words came back to me, bringing up the fact I hadn't eaten. But that was ridiculous. I'd been through hell; so what if I didn't have an appetite? I still had a pulse, didn't I? And I was breathing too. That pretty much shot the whole vampire thing straight to hell and meant that— for all I knew—I was just some pawn in their fucked-up game.

Trap a girl in your house. Convince her she's a vampire.

Maybe she'll sleep with you too.

A hysterical noise left me. Okay, so none of them had pressured me for sex. Or even broached the subject. Or looked like they really wanted that, considering how Liam had retreated rather than come closer when I was laid out on a bed right in front of him. And never mind the fact they probably weren't responsible for the fantasies that flooded my head or the way I...

God, I *craved* them.

My heart raced, the feeling distant and thready from my fear. Ulysses had put a bunch of memories in my head, though. Maybe he put this need for them in there too.

Except, again, not a single guy had acted on it.

I cursed at myself as I reached the double doors. Who cared if I was attracted to those men? Who cared about any of this? It didn't mean what they said about me was real.

The handles wouldn't budge.

"Dammit!" I kicked the door.

Nothing changed.

Muttering furiously about demons and delusional hotties, I spun and took off back down the hall, turning at the first corner I saw. Closed doors flanked me, and none of them opened when I twisted their handles. There wasn't a single window to be seen, as if the whole building was a fortress with me trapped inside.

"Let me out, damn you!" I shouted at the empty air.

Great. Now I was yelling at the house.

Snarling curses, I rounded another corner, and at the end of the hall, I spotted Asher through an open doorway.

A space surrounded him that looked like a conservatory, except all the windows were covered and not a single one of the countless plants along the walls was in bloom. A golden chandelier hung from the cathedral ceiling, casting light down on the white marble floor.

But the place had windows, and that's all that mattered.

"Asher!"

He turned at my shout, giving me a curious look as I hurried toward him.

"I need your help."

He tensed, and it suddenly occurred to me he might think I was asking him for what Gideon had tried to offer.

"I need you to open the window," I clarified. "I want to prove to you I can handle the sun, so then we can go find my sister. Deal?"

He eyed me for a moment. "Bringing you with us into a potential fight with rabids is not up for debate."

"If these things have her, then you showing up will just scare her more. You need me."

"And if this bond is intact and they kill you? All of us could end up dead."

God, they really believed that, didn't they? "But..." I floundered for another argument. "What if the fact I'm there is the only reason she comes with you to safety?" Or whatever this place was. "She's got to be terrified, Asher. She could run. I can't just sit here and risk that."

Letting out a breath, he looked away.

"Please."

"We test this first, then decide." His eyes met mine with a pointed look. "Deal?"

Relief shot through me. Finally, progress. I nodded fast.

Echoing the motion, he turned and crossed to an open space between two large marble planters. The walls were nothing but glass around us, but on their other side, a hard piece of what appeared to be plastic filled the casement as if it'd slid down from above, sealing out the sunlight completely.

"If you guys can handle the sun," I asked. "Why have the protective covering?"

"It's still draining. And we have guests from time to time who might be harmed."

I nodded. A weird anxiety was starting to thrum through me. Of course I was going to be fine when he cracked that seal. It was just the discovery of things other than humans in the world that was messing with my head.

Frowning for a heartbeat, Asher hesitated, and then suddenly a knife appeared in his grip. I blinked, trepidation flashing through me in spite of myself. I still had no explanation for that thing. It simply *appeared*, never mind how that should be impossible. The long metal blade seemed to catch every scrap of light from the chandelier above us, and something about it made me want to reach out to take it, though of course that was also nuts.

Taking a breath, he cranked the glass windowpane open to give him access to the protective shield over the window. He positioned his knife blade at the edge of the plastic and the casement, and then he paused, a flash of concern passing over his face.

"Please, Asher," I said.

He nodded again. "Step back."

I did.

Carefully, he wedged the blade below the plastic and then twisted, pushing the shield up ever so slightly.

A beam of sunlight pierced the conservatory, lighting a patch of the floor several feet away from me and making gold flecks glisten in the white marble. After so long in the dimness of the house, I winced a bit at the brightness.

Asher glanced at me. "Ready?"

Anxiety made my lungs struggle to take in much air, but I nodded all the same. "Ready."

I thrust my arm into the small beam of light.

I might as well have stuck myself into a fire.

With a shriek, I yanked my arm back, watching in horror as my skin began to crackle and burn. Pain raged from the wound, nearly blinding me with its intensity. I stumbled, but Asher was there before I fell, catching me.

He shouted, but the words were a blur beneath the rush of agony. Before my eyes, my skin was turning to ash. Inside the wound, the tendons and bones of my arm glowed as if they were embers in a fire. I was like wood, my core going up in flames. And it was spreading, turning my skin black, chewing down into my hand and up toward my elbow.

Bringing more pain than I'd ever felt in my life.

A splash of water landed on me, barely dulling the agony, and then the blur of a watering can tumbled away. Asher was speaking, but I couldn't hear him. This hurt too much. How could it hurt *this* much?

Suddenly, the ground lurched away as he hefted me up into his arms and raced from the room. Through the haze of agony, I could hear him continuing to shout, and other voices were there too now. But I couldn't make out the words because everything hurt. I was burning. All of me, burning from the sunlight's touch.

Because I was a vampire.

It was real. All of it. I'd died for three nights and come back as a thing from storybooks. I'd drank blood and probably would need to again. Except I wouldn't get the chance.

Because the sunlight was killing me.

I felt Asher lay me down on something soft. He moved away and then a new blur arrived. In words I couldn't understand, a soothing voice spoke to me, but I recognized the sound. Friday. A cool sensation touched my shoulder, and I whimpered. The feeling sank into my skin like ice penetrating my bones, spreading as she continued down my arm.

Until the heat vanished completely.

My arm felt dead. I was afraid to check whatever remained of it.

And I wasn't breathing. I blinked, staring up at the curtains draped across the four-poster bed. I couldn't detect a trace of my own heartbeat. Everything was numb but not cold, as if I was sinking into ice but couldn't even feel it. Shadows swirled on the edges of my vision, bringing with them an exhaustion so complete, I was afraid if I succumbed to it, I'd never wake up.

Voices started to penetrate the haze. Arguing, but distant, like a thread of sound from beyond the horizon. Meanwhile, the silence around me was so pervasive, it was all I could really focus on.

How had I never realized I could hear the whisper of blood in my veins? Or the rush of air in my chest? Now, there was nothing. Just an emptiness so deep and wide, it could never hope to be filled.

"Wren?"

My eyes turned toward the sound of my name, finding Asher there. Blinking against the encroaching shadows, I managed to focus long enough to see the other three standing around the bed.

A low rumble entered my world, and it took me a moment to realize it came from me. A new heat spread through me, not of fire, or at least not the kind from the sun. My mouth felt strange, like something odd was happening to my teeth, but it barely registered against the moisture spreading between my legs and the way my breasts tingled with need for these men. On the duvet, my fingers fisted into the cloth, while my rumbling growl turned to a keening moan and my insides twisted with hunger and heat.

But the shadows were swelling higher, and even as I tried to reach for him, the exhaustion dragged me back down. Asher and the others blurred, their forms receding into nothing as the darkness swallowed me whole.

---

When I opened my eyes, the world was silent.

I lay on the bed, straining to hear, but there was nothing. My breath was gone. My heart hadn't started beating. The air itself was utterly still in a way that I suspected no one ever experienced.

No one living, anyway.

Cautiously, I lifted my arm, bracing myself for what I might see. My skin was deathly pale, a shade like no blood remained in my flesh at all. Where the sunlight had touched, a white bandage wrapped my arm, obscuring the damage I knew had to be under there, while thick cream peeked past the edges. A woven blanket covered the rest of me, as if someone hadn't wanted me to be cold, even though I couldn't feel a thing about the temperature around me.

A soft rustle came from my right, and I tensed, looking over.

Asher sat beside me.

My insides twisted, and I groaned, cringing in on myself and rolling away from him. Hunger gnawed at my middle until I felt hollow.

"Here," he said quietly.

I couldn't bring myself to look toward him.

"Wren."

At the command in his voice, I risked a glance over my shoulder. Eyeing me carefully, he lifted a plate from the nightstand. "It's not blood, but it will keep you going. Though, if you want the other..."

I cowered away from him, whimpering involuntarily. I wouldn't do that. Not when I'd already seen how Gideon felt about it. None of the others had been in any rush, either, and I wouldn't force someone, not if there was a damn thing I could do about it. The thought was sickening.

A sigh left him. "Eat this. Please?"

Something settled on the mattress, and my eyes twitched back toward it.

He'd set the plate on the duvet. Small cream-colored cubes sat on top of the porcelain saucer, their consistency appearing somewhere between marshmallows and rice. They resembled the things Liam had brought into the study an eternity ago, though I'd never gotten the chance to ask what in the world they were.

"Try it," he said.

I gave him a wary look. His brow rose, insistent.

Carefully, I reached out, my body quivering with the urge to grab his arm and pull him to me instead. The cube was warm when I touched it, but when I brought it back to my lips, I couldn't smell a thing about it.

Though that might have been because I wasn't breathing.

Closing my eyes, I forced myself to take a bite.

Flavors of steak and gravy and mashed potatoes flooded my mouth. My eyes flew open.

Asher's lip twitched. I paused, uncertain whether I'd ever seen him smile.

But it was beautiful.

"Not bad, eh?"

Quickly, I nodded and grabbed another one of the cubes. My hunger was fading, though my breath hadn't returned and my heart remained still. But I could think more clearly and the aching in my body wasn't as powerful.

"What is that?" I asked, my voice hoarse.

"We call them snack cubes. Not a particularly original description, but accurate."

"But what... I mean, what are they?"

"A creation by some of our kind. Give food scientists a few centuries of lifespan and it's amazing what they come up with. As for the details..." He shrugged. "Humans can make milk from oats and cheese from cashews now. I suspect this is similar—after a fashion."

I hesitated mid-motion, my fingers just shy of picking up another cube.

"They're safe," he assured me. "We use them frequently when we need to keep moving but don't want to feed."

I shifted uncomfortably on the duvet. "And how..." I cleared my throat. "How often do you need to do that?"

He was silent for a moment. "You'll need to soon, Wren. You might have made it another week, but with that wound..." A grimace twisted his face as he looked away. "I'm sorry. I shouldn't have risked you like that. Given what we feel around you, I believed the bond would protect you, but obviously, I was mistaken."

Something in my chest ached, even if I couldn't feel my heart beating at all. The guilt on his face was horrible, but so was the fact this almost certainly meant I wasn't anything to them.

Just as Gideon had said.

I drew the blanket up higher, trying to shove the pointless ache away. "It's okay. I asked you to do it."

His gaze flicked back up to mine.

My shoulder rose and fell. "I didn't really believe I was... you know."

A hint of his smile returned. "Takes some getting used to."

I looked away. "So, is the rest of it true, then? Garlic and crucifixes and—" My eyes snapped back to him, a new thought suddenly occurring to me. "How old are you?"

Blowing out a breath, he rubbed his palms against his thighs. "I'll be nine hundred and twenty-four this winter."

My mouth opened, closed, and then opened again. "A-and the others?"

His head bobbed to the side as he weighed his answer. "Liam is the youngest, as these things go. He's eight hundred and sixty. Gideon is a little older. Eight hundred and ninety-three. Ulysses is a little over a thousand years old." He paused. "He was with Amalie the longest."

A chill rolled through me. "Did she... I mean, was she the one who... you know?" I twitched a hand at him, not sure how to ask.

"Turned us?"

My head jerked in a tiny nod.

"Yes."

"I'm sorry."

He made a dismissing motion. "Wasn't you."

I looked back down at the plate. I knew what he said was true. In a way, burning in the sunlight had even proved it. Whatever remained of Amalie von Morgenstierne in my mind, it wasn't enough for me to survive the sun, let alone be anything else.

And that was good. Sort of, anyway. Except for the part where a beam of sunlight meant I could die. Or the one where it meant my connection to Asher and the others was probably just a remnant of the queen and nothing to do with me. I didn't want to have these men *chained* to me, and I didn't want to be a monster.

It just felt like a gulf had opened between me and the others that might be uncrossable. I couldn't deny I was drawn to them, intrigued by them, and ridiculously attracted to them. And the thought it was only Amalie in me causing all that...

Hurt.

"So now what?" I asked softly.

"We find your sister, wherever she is. We bring her back here and then... figure out what's next. The rabids are still after you. We need to know why."

I nodded. He sounded so definitive, like he knew exactly how to handle this, while I felt utterly out of my depth. "And you all leave me here?"

He hesitated. "It's the safest option."

I had no idea what to say. He was right. I burst into flames in the sun; they didn't. Harper had been kidnapped by creatures who probably couldn't handle the sun either, if Gideon was right that only the Sentinels had this power.

The four of them going now was strategically the best call and probably gave them an advantage in saving her, besides.

But I couldn't meet his eyes. My heart ached, and not just because I wanted to be out there helping to find my sister. I felt so distant from Asher right now in a way that didn't make sense. I didn't know any of these guys. Not really. Hell, they were nearly a millennium older than me, for God's sake. We had nothing in common except some nightmare relic in my mind that would destroy me given half the chance, not to mention how it *certainly* would hurt them.

But that didn't change anything. I still wanted to reach for him, and not just for sex or blood.

For contact.

"Wren," he said gently.

"You should probably go, then. Sunlight will give you an advantage, right?"

He was silent for a moment. "Yeah."

But he didn't move.

"Asher, you need to—"

"Does she look like you?"

My brow furrowed. "What?"

"Your sister. She's your twin, right?"

I hesitated. "Fraternal. We don't—"

"So the rabids could lie to us. Pass someone else off as your sister."

I looked up at him.

"We could probably use a picture of her, if you have one."

"Right." I moved to push the blanket aside, my body still feeling shaky. He rose swiftly, taking my arm to help me.

I froze. His hand felt warm against my skin, and even if I had been breathing, I certainly wouldn't have been able to in this moment.

Swallowing hard, I tried to order myself to move away, but nothing in my body was listening. I could feel his pulse through his fingertips on my arm, and I clamped my mouth shut against the soft sound of hunger that wanted to slip past my lips.

A breath left him. "It's okay."

My head shook, my eyes anywhere but on him.

"Wren—"

"I need to help Harper. And I'm not going to force you."

He was motionless for a moment, and then he sank down on the bed beside me. "What?"

"To do anything," I managed, unable to bring myself to say the exact words. "I'll figure it out. Maybe ask that doctor for more... you know. Or something. But I won't—"

"You're not forcing me."

"None of you want this, okay? I know that. I don't even want..." Pain twisted in my chest like a knife, making my voice thick. "Doesn't matter. I'm not going to *use* you."

A soft and disbelieving sound left him. I managed to pull back, putting cold distance between us like an icy expanse, even if he was only a few inches away.

"You're not her, Wren."

"I know."

And why did that hurt too?

I shifted slightly on the bed. It hurt because, if there really had been a connection between me and Asher, then maybe there could have been *more* than that between us as well.

Instead of nothing.

I didn't want to be that monster. But God help me if I didn't want to be with Asher and the others too.

His fingers took my chin, drawing my face back around toward him, and my insides quivered at the contact. "You're not her, so you're not using me. And you're not forcing me. I know the difference; trust me. It's why I brought the food here. I didn't want your hunger to force you, either."

A flower of gratitude blossomed in my chest, but uncertainty still filled me. "What if..." I struggled for the word. "What if *feeding* makes her stronger, though?"

He was silent for a moment. "It didn't when you first fed at the clinic. And you succumbing to starvation won't help anything."

There was that. "Gideon said—" I cleared my throat. "He told me that... it feels good."

Asher nodded, his fingers straying up to brush back a strand of my hair. My skin tingled where he touched. "It does. It can get pretty intense, though. Sexually, I mean. If you're attracted to the person you're with."

I could hear the question in his voice, and my eyes rose to his, desire pounding through me.

"Are you okay with that?" he asked softly.

I wetted my lips, and his gaze flicked down at the small motion. "I think so."

His eyes narrowed, questioning. He drew back slightly, caution on his face. "I won't do anything if you're not sure you want it, Wren. Not now or ever."

"I-I am. I mean... I just—" God, my body thrummed like tiny magnetic sparks filled the space between us, trying to draw me nearer to him. "I don't want to hurt you."

The corner of his lips rose. "You won't. You're..." He seemed to search for words for a moment. "You're letting me give you a gift."

Carefully, he held out his hand, and that deadly looking knife simply appeared, as if reality folded away, revealing it in his grasp. The blade glistened, dancing with blue-white flecks of light across the metal, though there wasn't any light like that in the room. I tensed when he moved the blade closer, but his eyes never left me and his expression was filled with nothing but reassurance. With a deft movement, he nicked a small line on the inside of his forearm, and blood welled from the cut.

A shudder ran through me. I couldn't take my eyes from the small slice of red on his skin, not even to watch his knife vanish again into nothing. A moan rose in my throat, and I clamped my mouth shut against it. The feeling that gripped me wasn't like before, wasn't crazed or uncontrollable, and I suspected I had Asher and the food he'd given me to thank for that.

But God, I still wanted this, and it terrified me.

His other hand rose, slipping along my cheek. "It's okay, Wren. I promise."

I trembled, unable to look away from the blood.

"You need your strength so you can be here for your sister when she comes back."

The words broke the blood's hold, making my gaze snap up to his. I hadn't considered that.

Oh God, what if I hurt Harper because I was too hungry to stop myself?

Gently, his hand on my cheek guided me toward the thin line of blood on his skin. "Let me help you."

My fingers took his forearm, and my eyes closed as he came near. Fighting back a wince, I hesitantly licked the wound.

Ambrosia.

Before I could even register the impulse, I'd gripped

his arm, my lips locked on the small, wonderful sips of ecstasy slipping from him into me. Everything fell away, from my awareness of the room to every inhibition, while energy poured into me like someone was injecting heat straight into my veins. I felt Asher shift around so his back was against the pillows, and immediately, I went with him, moving on top of him with scarcely a thought for how it left me pressed to every inch of his body.

A strange feeling filled my mouth, like something *right* sliding into place, and then his hand took my cheek.

"Here," he whispered.

He drew me away from his arm, bending his head to the side and exposing his throat, and utter instinct gripped me. I climbed higher along his body and bit down, my sharp fangs piercing his skin.

Pure life poured into me. Heat erupted in my veins, and my heart surged into action, pounding as every one of my senses suddenly exploded through me. His scent filled my lungs. His hot pulse beat beneath my lips, the rhythm nearly matching my own.

And his hard cock was under me, pressed against my hip.

Moaning against his skin, I ground myself on him, desire and need tangling inside me until I couldn't tell where one began and the other came to an end. Pleasure radiated from my clit and spread like wildfire through my veins as I worked myself against him. My craving for blood was fading, but another remained. I withdrew my fangs from his throat, licking his skin swiftly on some unknown impulse, and before my eyes, the wounds healed.

A hungry noise left him, and the flesh beneath my legs throbbed at the sound. My sharp teeth retracted as I moved quickly to his lips, kissing him. With one hand, he gripped the back of my head, holding me to him while his tongue plundered my mouth, and short begging noises escaped me as I pressed myself harder against his length. I wanted all of him. Everything. My God...

His other palm slid down my side and beneath the waistband of my jeans until he found my ass. My back arched, trying to give him more access to me, and he took me up on the invitation immediately, his hand continuing on until his fingers teased at my slick entrance.

I groaned. The sound seemed to send his desire flaming higher, and in a rush of motion, he flipped me, laying me on my back beneath him. Instantly, I reached for him, desperate to keep his mouth to mine. He slid his hand over my body, tangling briefly with the fastener of my jeans.

Oh, yes.

I moved fast, helping him push them down. His hand slipped between my legs, and I moaned as his fingers slid inside me and his thumb massaged my clit. God, I was so wet for him. Gasping, I writhed beneath his touch, pressing into his confident motions as he worked me, sending my pulse flying.

"More..." I breathed. "Oh, God, don't stop."

A pleased chuckle left him. His lips trailed hot kisses along my throat, and I tilted my head to the side, giving him access.

The instinctive motion sent a thrill through me. God, if he drank from me too...

My body thrummed with the desire for him to do just that.

But he didn't bite down, and in only a moment, incredible pressure began building through my body, radiating out from his steady motions and obliterating any trace of coherent thought.

"Asher... oh, God, Asher."

My breathing sped up, and my words disintegrated into urgent, pleading noises. Squeezing my eyes shut, I ground myself against his hand, praying he didn't stop. How the hell he was making me feel this way with only his fingers was beyond me. And God, to think what it'd be like if his cock was inside me instead...

Tension built inside me. The world came down to his lips on my throat, nipping at me. His amazing body above me. And the feeling of him massaging me harder... harder...

The orgasm erupted through me, and I cried out, my muscles clenching around his fingers and my body overcome by the waves of pleasure rolling through me. And there was only us. Only his touch and the overwhelming bliss of what he'd just done to me. My breath came in rapid gasps and my heart thudded fast in my chest as the aftershocks faded, and opening my eyes, I looked up to find him smiling at me, satisfaction clear in his expression.

I couldn't help but return his smile. My hand slid down between us, finding the fastener for his pants, and desire darkened his eyes. I could feel his hard length against my hip, and I was desperate to have him inside me, just as I'd been fantasizing about since practically the moment I laid eyes on him. I craved his cock filling me, thrusting into me. I wanted his hands on my breasts. Memory told me what an incredible lover he was. How he could make me feel, and I—

My motions stopped. Trembling crept through me.

"Wren, what is it?"

I could barely form the words. "How... how do I know this is me?"

He pulled back slightly, his eyes meeting mine with concern. "How do you feel?"

My gaze skipped around while I searched inside myself for the answer. "Good... I think."

A smile crossed his face.

I wanted to smile back but worry paralyzed me. Could I trust this? Trust what I felt when the thoughts that had just flashed through my head weren't really even mine?

Asher drew back a bit more, and guilt joined my worry. He'd done all that for me, and now I was going to leave him without any release.

I reached for the fastener on his pants again.

His hand caught mine. "Hey."

I looked up at him.

He gave me a reassuring look. "I'm okay. Are you?"

I swallowed hard. I didn't know how to answer that. It was true I felt more stable than I had in a while. My heart was beating stronger; my lungs were taking in more air. But that wasn't all of it. There was something... more. Like, if the draw I'd felt to Asher previously had been background noise in my mind, it was somehow clearer now.

But was that a connection between us or just my imagination?

Or the queen?

My other hand found the necklace Eden had given me, and I gripped it like it was a lifeline. "Are you sure you're okay?" I asked.

He nodded, gentle thoughtfulness in his expression like I'd just done something special, even if I didn't quite understand what. "Yeah."

His hand reached out, taking mine. A shuddering breath entered my lungs. My body still ached to have him, and I would have given anything to be able to return to what we'd been doing.

But fear still drummed through me.

And that didn't even bring into it all the time I'd already taken.

"Harper," I said. "We need to... or *you* need to... you know."

He sighed, squeezing my hand. "Yeah."

Was that a touch of regret in his voice?

But then he smiled and lifted my hand to his lips, kissing it gently like some knight from a fairy tale. "But if you need anything—" His eyes strayed downward and then returned to my own, full of meaning. "I'm here."

I couldn't even speak. My body started to burn with desire all over again, while my mind couldn't quite let go of the fear it wasn't really me craving him. Not fully.

Unsteadily, I managed a nod.

He echoed the motion more firmly, giving me a smile. "Let's get your sister back to you."

**23**

---

ASHER

I hadn't wanted anyone this badly in all my nine hundred plus years.

While Wren climbed to her feet and straightened her clothes, I made myself take a steadying breath and willed my cock to calm down. Gods below, that had been even more incredible than I could have imagined, having her feed from me, work herself on me, open herself to me like she had. I'd never felt anything like that in my life, and if her fear—understandable though it was—hadn't brought everything to a stop, I'd probably still have her on that bed, sweat coating her soft skin as I brought her to orgasm after orgasm.

My eyes strayed over her again, watching her while her back was turned. I wouldn't make a move unless she was ready for it, but the moment she was...

I scrubbed a hand over my face quickly, ordering myself to get a grip on anything besides her beautiful curves. Her sister was out there, possibly in the hands of rabids, and there was no telling what they'd do to the girl.

I didn't leave innocents behind, even if I didn't know them, and *especially* when they mattered to those I cared about.

Wren glanced back at me, and I gave her a smile I hoped was reassuring. I did care about her, I realized. More than just because it was right or she needed help, but because, in every way, she was the antithesis of the cruelty and sadism we'd survived. Her passion for helping others was unmistakable. She'd rather starve than hurt someone and rather suffer than cause anyone pain. The mere thought she'd be using me had been enough to stop her from feeding, even though her hunger must have been incredible.

She was so committed to keeping me and everyone around her safe, and the truth of that made me want to do whatever it took to be certain she always stayed safe as well.

And stayed with us.

I followed her to the door. The others were torn, I knew that. Gideon still saw her as a potential monster. Ulysses was haunted by all Amalie had done. Liam, I suspected, had trusted Wren first, but being with her would still be difficult for him. And there were, of course, Wren's feelings to consider. Would she want all of us? Was she drawn to each of us too?

Air escaped me. I could only hope. If there was any chance we could have her and expel the traces of Amalie, I wanted us to take it.

Because I never wanted Wren to be away from us, not if she could be convinced to stay.

We made our way downstairs, though I noted that Friday or Barnaby had shifted the location of several doors along the corridor. They were closer now, even if I suspected our rooms beyond hadn't changed. A message, perhaps? The two of them playing matchmaker with us all?

I wouldn't be surprised. The demons occasionally acted like concerned grandparents, worrying about the four of us and hinting at how it wasn't good for us to be alone.

When we reached the first floor, I could hear voices from the study across the hall, and I headed that way.

Behind me, Wren's steps slowed, and I glanced back, confused. Trepidation showed on her face.

"What's wrong?" I asked, returning to her.

Her gaze darted to the open door of the study. "I guess... they'll know, won't they? About..." She twitched her head in the general direction of the stairs to the upper floors, and her eyes couldn't quite meet mine.

"Yes," I admitted. "Most likely."

She looked uncomfortable.

"You needed to feed, Wren. And as for the others... They would be wise not to judge either of us, as I—" A smile pulled at my lips. "I truly wanted to do that with you. When and if you would ever choose it, I'd like to do quite a bit more."

Pink spread through her cheeks. I reached out, taking her hand and squeezing it. She drew a breath, nodding wordlessly.

We walked into the study.

Liam and Gideon looked up from a map they had spread across the desk, while over by the shuttered windows, Ulysses paused mid-sentence on a phone call. Their eyes flashed between me and Wren, and despite what I'd said, I tensed, wondering what their reactions would truly be.

For a moment, none of them said a word.

"I think I have a lead," Ulysses spoke into the silence.

A short breath left Wren.

"I called a few of my contacts. They reported a band of rabids north of town. Don't seem to be in any hurry to move on, either."

"That tracks with the potential sightings among the dormants," Gideon added.

Wren glanced between us. "Dormants?"

"Civilian vampires," I explained. "They don't feed on humans but stick to blood bags and the like. Basically, the ones who pass as human in society."

She blinked. "But they've seen some of these... rabids?"

I glanced at Gideon.

His head inclined slightly. "They believe so."

"So, now what?" Wren asked.

"We do some reconnaissance," I said. "See if we can't find signs of where they—"

The phone on the desk rang.

I looked between the others, finding the same wariness on their faces as I knew had to be on my own. Friday had only manifested that phone today, when Wren said she needed one. I doubted it even had a real phone number.

"Is someone going to answer that?" Wren prompted.

Maybe it did, though. Maybe this was a misdial or some telemarketer looking to sell us timeshares. As it rang again, I reached out, taking the brass receiver and lifting it cautiously to my ear.

"Sentinel," came a gravelly voice on the other end.

Shit. So much for the hope this was an innocent mistake. "Who is this?"

A chuckle answered me, and the sound made my skin crawl. Rabid. He had to be.

"One of many, Sentinel. *Legion*."

I glanced at the others, cursing the fact this old-style phone didn't have a speaker function.

But then that would only mean Wren could hear this crazy-sounding bastard.

"We know you have the girl," the rabid continued. "We know you want the one we have too. So I have a proposal. Midnight. Neuhaus Cemetery. You bring your girl and the other one lives. If you come alone or leave her hiding somewhere we can't see her?" He chuckled again. "You'll be telling that sweet thing all about how her sister got her throat ripped out and died choking on her own blood."

Rage rolled through me, and my hand clenched down on the phone.

"So, Sentinel. What's it going to be?" The man laughed, and then a click came from the phone as he hung up.

For a moment, I didn't move. Wren's sister might be dead already. This could easily be a trap. And Neuhaus

Cemetery was at least an hour away, meaning it'd be nearly dark by the time we made it there, anyway.

Dammit.

"What was that?" Wren asked nervously.

Carefully, I set the receiver back in place before looking over at her and then onward to the others. We couldn't bring Wren. It wasn't an option.

But if her sister *wasn't* dead yet, then I didn't doubt for a second the rabid would do as he said.

"We need to talk for a minute," I said to Wren. "Could you...?"

She blinked. "What? Go wait outside?" I started to speak, but she cut me off. "No. *Hell*, no. I may not know much about your world, but keeping things from me isn't helping anything. I'm not letting you kick me out like some kid."

A grimace pulled at my face. "We—"

"This is Harper we're talking about. If you have news concerning her, then it concerns me too."

"I'm just trying to protect you," I argued.

Wren shook her head. "Protect *her*."

I stared at her for a moment. Determination was written in every line of her body, and I got the impression that—even if I were to try to stick her in the hall—she'd break down the door to get back inside.

A strange feeling spread through me. Gods below, in spite of myself... I was impressed.

"They have your sister," I said. "It's broad daylight out there, which means we can't fly, and she's almost an hour's ride away. And if we don't bring you where they can see you, they'll kill her."

A swift gulp was Wren's only reaction. "Then I guess I need to come too, don't I?"

Her voice was like iron.

"If we bring you," Gideon stated. "We'll have to wait until full nightfall before we even start out. She'll only be in their hands even longer." His attention flicked to me. "If we make them wait, they could kill the girl."

Wren shook her head. "Test me again."

"What?" Ulysses set down his cell phone, taking a step toward her before seeming to catch himself. "You could have *died*, and you want to—"

"I said test me again." Her eyes snapped over to him, furious.

He froze.

"You already established that our bond isn't with you," Gideon countered. "Immolating yourself a second time helps nothing. Leaving you here and going now is the best option."

"We don't know the bond isn't there," I snapped while Wren blinked, looking away.

Gideon regarded me flatly. "I take it she fed, then."

I bristled at the hint of contempt in his voice. "I asked her to. And she damn near didn't anyway."

Gideon's eye narrowed at the insinuated accusation in my tone.

"We're wasting time." Wren headed for the window on the other side of the study, pausing only long enough to snag a letter opener from the shelf.

Alarm shot through me at the realization she meant to pry the protective shield open herself. I rushed after her, but Liam got there first, catching her arm and shaking his head insistently.

Wren tugged at his grasp. "I'm not waiting around while—"

"You don't have to," I interrupted. "But if you push the shield too far loose and you're not safe in the sun, you could combust before we could save you."

Hesitancy flickered over her face. I summoned my knife from the ether and motioned for her to step back. "Please?"

She retreated.

Exhaling to steady myself, I paused at the point of prying back the shield. I couldn't believe I was doing this again. Nearly killing her once wasn't good enough?

But then, I could read the determination returning to her face. If I didn't do this, she'd probably find a door and try to test herself that way.

And then we could come back to find nothing but a pile of ash.

Dammit.

I glanced over my shoulder. Gideon was already at the study entrance telling Friday to get another first aid kit. Liam was watching us both like a hawk, while Ulysses appeared nauseated.

"Get ready to grab her if this goes wrong," I said to them.

Ulysses nodded and started forward, only to have Liam move faster and take his place by her side. His mouth tightening, Ulysses stepped back again.

I ignored the silent exchange. I wasn't sure any of us were over what Ulysses had done to her—never mind how Wren might be feeling about it all—but right now, it wasn't the most important thing.

"Ready?" I asked, directing the question to Liam as much as her.

They both nodded.

I inserted the blade into the crack between the shield and the casement and twisted sharply. A sliver of sunlight pierced the room, deep gold from the late afternoon hour.

Wren drew a deep breath and then stuck her uninjured arm out quickly. Instantly, she tensed, wincing.

But she didn't burst into flames.

The sunlight passed over her forearm, wisps of smoke rising for a moment, and then her skin shimmered like she'd been burnished by gold. As if a fire had been extinguished, the smoke faded and then the gold effect did too, leaving only her unmarked skin.

Air left her as she drew her arm back again.

"How do you feel?" I asked.

"Fine." She sounded breathless. Carefully, she brushed her fingertips over her forearm. "Totally fine."

Her eyes lifted from her skin, and she stared at us all. The air felt like it was charged, and the tension made the hairs on the back of my neck rise. This proved the bond between us persisted. That more could be to come.

If she gained this ability merely by feeding on me, what could feeding on each of us do?

Or more than feeding...

She drew a breath, seeming shaken. "I guess this means we should go, then."

Pushing the thoughts away, I managed a nod. If she

was safe in the sun, there was no way she'd stay put here, regardless of what we said.

At least with us, she would be protected.

"You have any practice with weapons?" Gideon asked her, his voice tight. He'd come to the same conclusion. I'd bet on it.

Wren shook her head.

Tossing me a glare as if blaming me for the entire situation, he yanked open the door. "Then we better see if Friday can conjure you some armor."

**24**

---

WREN

I looked like a biker chick who'd gotten a *little* too excited over Kevlar.

Surreptitiously adjusting my new leather jacket, I followed the guys toward the door. A bulletproof vest covered my chest, and the coat had layers of bullet-proofing woven into it as well, apparently as a defense against magical bullets. My pants were likewise made of leather with Kevlar patches sewn in along my thighs and shins. Black boots with steel toes clunked when I walked, and a thick collar wrapped my neck—protection against biting and beheading alike. The guys were similarly dressed, but on them, the whole ensemble looked badass.

Meanwhile I felt like a kid playing dress-up.

Friday extended a helmet to me when we reached the door. I balked. "I can't—"

"For the ride," she interrupted.

I blinked as Ulysses pulled open the door. Four motor-cycles stood beyond it, on the opposite side of what appeared to be a weathered porch. I followed the others out the door, glancing back while I descended the steps.

The house was a crumbling manor with broken shutters and moss growing up the decayed columns of the porch. There was even a blue tarp over a nearby window and a rusted light dangling from a rat's nest of wires beside the door. But even as I looked at it all, my eyes wanted to go anywhere else, a sickened feeling twisting in my stomach like being within a hundred miles of this place was a bad idea. "What the…"

"We keep a low profile, remember?" Friday said from the entryway. Beyond her, what had been an enormous hall of marble and polished wood now looked like a shadowy stretch of rotting boards and snarled cobwebs, complete with holes in the walls and a mouse industriously making its way across the dirty floor.

With a smile, Friday shut the door.

I faltered, feeling like reality had gone a bit unreliable on me. Nothing I saw should have been possible, but then, that description could fit just about everything from these past few days. Men who turned into smoke? Check. A witch in the woods? No problem. Demons who commanded a house that could materialize rooms at random and look like two utterly different places depending upon which side of the front door you stood?

Yeah, sure. Whatever.

"You coming?" Gideon snapped.

I flinched when Asher's hand took my elbow, and I swallowed hard as I managed a nod. I'd left Wonderland to join a vampire motorcycle gang on their way to rescue my sister from monsters.

Who needed reality anyway?

---

Trees lined the road to the cemetery, and before we even reached it, the other three guys split off on their bikes, driving away along nearby side roads like they were on some predetermined route. Clutching my arms around Asher's waist, I kept silent, worried that any sound over the rumble of his bike might cause an attack.

My eyes darted to the swiftly darkening sky past the smoked visor of my helmet. The guys could fly, and the creatures who attacked me that night on the cliff had snatched me out of midair. Could all vampires do that?

Could I?

My arms tightened on Asher as if gravity might suddenly lose its hold on me entirely.

We crested the rise, and the cemetery came into view, a sprawl of green grass climbing a gentle slope ringed by trees and a low wall of roughhewn stone. An iron archway hung over the entrance, and the intricately twisted gate stood open to the road outside it.

My gaze tracked over the rows upon rows of granite and marble gravestones, all of them arrayed before an ornate mausoleum at the top of the hill. Harper would be alive. Somewhere in that field of death, she would be fine and safe and entirely alive.

Even if I couldn't see where she was right now.

A trembling breath left me as Asher sent the motorcycle down the hill toward the gate. My eyesight felt torn, as if it was struggling between normal human vision and that strange, silvered glow I'd seen on everything several nights before. Details shimmered, appearing normal and then decidedly not, and the effect made it hard for me to focus.

But maybe that was the point. Maybe these *rabids,* whatever they were, had chosen this time for exactly that reason.

Asher came to a stop at the gate. "Stay behind me and stay close," he said to me, his attention on scanning our surroundings. "But if I tell you to run, you do it no matter what's happening, understand?" He glanced at me over his shoulder.

I gave a tight nod. "Where would they have her?"

He paused as, in the distance, the rumble of motorcycles came from either side. The others, I hoped.

"Not sure," he answered me. "Probably the mausoleum."

Something about the way he said it left "if she's still alive" hanging in the air.

I shivered. She would be. We'd find her.

Muttering to himself in a language I didn't recognize, Asher drove the motorcycle past the gates of the cemetery.

Even the air was still as we rolled along the pale gravel track between the graves. Names scrolled past me, meaningless because they weren't hers. Bright splashes of loving tributes clustered randomly at the sides of the markers—fake flowers, a wreath, a child's stuffed toy.

I turned away, locking my gaze on the mausoleum. She'd be in there, safe, and everything would be fine.

A rumble of another motorcycle came from beyond the small building, and a moment later, Liam pulled around the corner along where the track looped the marble structure. I couldn't see Gideon or Ulysses, but I could guess they were watching from somewhere beneath the trees around the cemetery.

Without a word, Asher stopped the bike and waited as Liam swung off the machine and walked toward the door.

My fingers dug into Asher's leather jacket. Shadows hung thick over the mausoleum. The sunlight was fading; at any moment, it would be gone entirely.

With a soft click, Liam unlatched the lock. Hinges creaked as the door swung open.

The small building was empty.

A desperate breath left me, and my eyes darted over the graveyard. "Where is she? If she's not here, then—"

I froze. Where the hill began to slope back down again, beside an enormous tree, there was a pile of disturbed dirt.

And everything in me knew.

I scrambled off the bike, ignoring Asher's alarmed protest. Marble graves and bright tributes flashed past me, blurring and pointless, and then I was there, tumbling to my knees beside the mound of dark earth, my fingers ripping through it.

Bloodless skin.

Golden hair.

No.

A cry ripped from me as I uncovered Harper's face. She wasn't moving and her eyes were closed, and when I touched her face, her skin was ice cold. A bruise stained her cheek like a blue-purple ghost, traveling up past her hairline where it met a gash like she'd been hit with something.

But they would have bitten her. Like me, they would've bitten her, and so she'd be back again and fine and—

"Wren." Asher's hand took my shoulder.

I looked up at him. "When will she wake up?"

He hesitated.

"Asher, when?"

"Three nights. Maybe. But…"

"What?"

His pained expression sent ice racing through me. "Rabids don't usually turn people, Wren."

Shoving his hand away, I scrambled to my feet, putting myself between him and Harper. "They did with me."

"That was extremely rare. They're predators, nothing more. They don't—"

"She's my sister, and they bit me, so they must have bitten her—" Movement caught the corner of my eye, and I turned quickly.

Liam bent over Harper. For only a moment, he shifted into shadows and swept across her, pushing all the dirt away.

A sob choked me. Her fingernails were raw, like they'd been ripped away, and her knuckles were too, as if she'd been punching at something. Livid marks wrapped her wrists and ankles, showing where she'd probably been bound. Dirt stained her clothes from head to toe, and one of her shoes was missing.

But all of it paled in comparison to the stab wound right at her heart.

Stupid, pointless tears burned in my eyes, and I

couldn't breathe around the scream trapped in my throat. This wasn't real. It couldn't be.

Swiftly, Liam checked over her, only to glance back at Asher with a solemn look on his face. "No bites," he rasped.

My head shook. "No. No, they... they would've... They bit me. They've would've bitten—"

"I'm sorry." Asher's voice was pained.

"Can you?" I ripped my gaze from my sister to stare at him. "Bite her, I mean? Can you—"

Asher's sorrowful expression was my answer. "From the look of that wound... She's been dead for hours, Wren. There's no one left to bring back."

My mouth moved, torn between pleading and a howl of agony. We'd been too late. Too late when I burned myself with the sun. Too late when I drank blood just to come save her.

Too late, too late.

Liam bent down again, working his hands beneath Harper's body to lift her from the ground. Her limbs were stiff and didn't move right, and the sight twisted my gut.

But she wouldn't stay that way. She wouldn't. Three nights from now, she'd wake up just like I did, and every-thing would be—

Something shot past me in a flash of silver, moving so fast it ripped through the strands of my hair.

A spear impaled Liam, sending him crashing back-ward. Harper's body tumbled from his arms. Before I could even scream, Asher whipped around me, turning instantly to shadow. Wind rushed past as he carried me to the side of the mausoleum, and then he shifted back to human form the moment my back hit the marble.

I couldn't take my eyes from Liam. Where he lay on the grass, the silver spear protruded up like a grave marker all its own. Around us, shrieks rose from beneath the trees on either side of the cemetery, and the sounds of fighting followed. A dull throb pounded through my body, strengthening when Asher grabbed my arm, pulling me with him along the side of the mausoleum.

"Fuck, fuck, *fuck!*" Asher muttered under his breath. I glanced at him and gasped.

His face was tight as if he was struggling against pain, and his teeth were bared, fangs showing.

"Gideon is down too," he snarled. "Those *bastards.* Where the hell did they get—"

Darkness erupted at the edge of the cemetery, rushing out from beneath the trees like the deepening night had taken on a life of its own.

Ulysses crashed down beside us. A bloody gash showed on his forehead, and one of his arms was dripping. "Too many of the fuckers." He jerked his head toward the gate. "Take her. I'll cover you."

My mouth dropped open. "But you—"

Asher didn't wait. Shifting back to shadow, he engulfed me, and the ground dropped away.

"Dammit, we can't leave them!" I shouted at Asher. "They—"

My words died in a shriek as he suddenly dove. Metal flashed overhead, a spear darting through the space where we'd been. Dark and amorphous shapes raced from the cemetery while more surged in on all sides.

Something collided with us from above, slamming into Asher and sending me tumbling. I crashed back down to the earth, rolling until I hit the marble slab of a gravestone.

Snarls came from above, and I looked up just in time to see a thrashing tangle of shadows careening straight toward me. Scrambling out of the way, I crawled behind another marble slab as the one where I'd been only a moment before toppled with the impact of the fighting vampires.

"Run, Wren!" Asher shouted, shifting briefly to human form and then lunging at the monsters again.

Another shadow surged toward me, shifting to Ulysses at the last moment. "Come on!"

He snagged my wrist, pulling me toward him. At lightning speed, he shifted again, scooped me up, and took off across the graveyard, sticking close to the ground. Like a mad slalom race, he wove us between the graves toward the gate.

We didn't make it far.

Waves of shrieking shadows raced toward us, tearing into him and sending me crashing to the ground again only a few yards from the cemetery gate. Ulysses shifted back quickly, putting himself between me and the shadows, while his knife suddenly appeared in his grasp. Barely taking his eyes from the amorphous monsters rushing toward us, he reached back.

And shoved the hilt into my hand.

I froze, alarmed.

"Keep it," he snapped. "Run like hell and stab anything that gets close, got it?"

My fingers wrapped around the cool hilt. A shiver like a faint electrical charge raced from my palm to my arm. The knife felt... good. Right.

Ulysses threw a swift glance at me. "Dammit, run!"

The shadows struck him. He shifted fast, and shrieks rose as he tore into them. Like a deadly ghost, he ripped through them, annihilating any that tried to reach me.

My hand tightened on the hilt. I didn't want to leave him. Any of them.

But they couldn't get out of here if they were busy defending me.

I took off, racing past the gate while monsters howled in my wake.

## 25

ASHER

My blade slashed through the rabid, and the energy of the knife shifted with me as I changed form, becoming a weapon of shadow just as much as I was. The rabids died screaming, their amorphous bodies disintegrating as I tore through them, but still there were more of them. Countless more.

Gods below, where the hell had all these bastards come from? I hadn't thought there were this many rabids left in the state. Hell, the *country*.

In the distance, I spotted Ulysses grabbing Wren. Blurring into shadow, he took off, carrying her away from this madness.

Thank the gods.

Except all the rabids followed him.

I hesitated, torn. Everything in me howled with the need to go help them. Protect Wren. But if we lost Liam or Gideon, we might be too weakened to help her.

Shit.

I shifted form for speed and raced past the mausoleum. On the ground, Liam lay, that damned spear straight through his chest. Wren's sister was beside him, her limbs awkward and stiff from death.

And if I didn't move quickly, Liam would join her.

Shifting back fast, I crouched by his side and checked him over swiftly. His chest was still, but I could feel that he wasn't fully dead. Beneath the trees beyond the cemetery, Gideon was the same. Clinging to life. Racked with pain.

Gods help me, it made it hard to think like a man and not a wounded beast.

Gritting my teeth, I gripped the spear. The enchanted silver steamed against my hand, chewing into my skin. Where the hell the rabids had gotten such a thing, I had no idea. This kind of metalworking had been lost centuries ago, and the last thing I expected was for a bunch of decaying rabids to be wielding the thing.

With a sharp yank, I ripped the spear from his chest and then tossed it away as fast as I could.

Burn marks scored my palm, but I ignored them, crouching over my friend. "Come on, Liam. Come on."

My awareness of his life force began to fade.

"*Fuck!*" I ripped my fangs across my scorched palm and then pressed the bloody gash to his chest right above the wound. So soon after feeding Wren, this would cost me, but not as much as his death would. There wasn't another option.

And I'd gladly spend eternity on my death bed if it kept these men alive.

Casting a quick look around, I checked that the rabids were still busy elsewhere, and then I closed my eyes, focusing on sending my energy to Liam along the bond between us.

His life force strengthened like heat gathering beneath my palm.

Gasping with relief, I drew my hand away and opened my eyes. He stirred, pushing up from the ground. No air entered his lungs, and I knew his heart wouldn't be beating, not in this state. His skin was like snow and his eyes glinted like shards of ice, his gaze more animal than rational as it swept the cemetery. "Wren?" he rasped like a threat to anything that had dared touch her.

"She's in trouble," I said. "Go help Gideon and then get back here."

He nodded once and then vanished into shadow and raced toward the trees.

I turned, scanning the graveyard.

Ulysses was under attack.

And Wren was nowhere to be seen.

Swearing vehemently, I shifted and sped across the cemetery, slashing into the rabids the moment I reached them. The creatures shrieked like wild animals, their amorphous forms turning to tattered darkness and dust as they died.

But still they kept coming. Dozens of them now, rather than the hundreds from before, tearing at us like monsters from nightmares, all claws and teeth amid black formlessness. In shadow form, Ulysses spun behind me, ripping through the bastards who tried to circle us, while I surged upward, slicing through the ones who came from above.

Beyond the cluster attacking us, more rabids were racing for the road leading away from the cemetery.

That had to be where Wren had gone.

*This way,* I sent to Ulysses before taking off after them. He slashed through a rabid and followed.

*She has my knife,* he sent back. *Keep going west. It's there.*

Surprise hit me, followed by relief. Our blades were part of us, summoned from the ether, tied to our souls. We never gave them up. And if his blade was anywhere on earth, Ulysses could find it.

Which meant he could find her too.

In the distance at my back, I felt Gideon's life force strengthen. A moment later, he and Liam were racing toward us.

My relief grew, tingeing the edge of my adrenaline rush. At least they were alive. Yet, whatever trace of the bond had been strengthened by Wren feeding on me, it wasn't enough to tell me the same about her.

Or whether we'd make it to her in time.

## 26

---

### WREN

There was no way I could move faster than a flying shadow.

Something slammed into me before I'd made it a dozen yards past the cemetery gate, and instantly, I knew it wasn't one of the Sentinels. Snarling at me like a wild dog, the monster ripped me away from the ground and took to the air. I tried to scream, but darkness flooded my mouth, tasting like rotted meat and sodden dirt, choking my cry. The creature's hold shifted on me, twisting my knife hand behind my back where I couldn't lash out, and pain shot through my shoulder and arm. Only sheer willpower kept me from dropping the blade. With my free hand, I thrashed, frantically trying to break free, but there was nothing to hit. Just formless darkness that gave like I was punching a cloud whenever my fist struck it.

A ragged laugh reached my ears as the creature

climbed higher into the sky, the sound raw like a rattle from a corpse.

Rage surged through me. The thing was *enjoying* this. It liked me fighting and failing. It liked my desperate attempts to break free.

Had it enjoyed Harper's struggle too? Had this thing laughed at my sister before it or one of its buddies stabbed her in the heart?

Absolute hate poured through me, bright like a fire fit to set my bones alight. These things had killed my sister. They'd put a spear through Liam and maybe killed him too.

And they were *laughing* at me.

A scream ripped from me, and my body flew apart with it. Everything in me seemed to explode outward, shattering my human form, turning it to darkness and shadow.

And pure fury.

I tore into the monster holding me. The knife was gone from my fist, but somehow, the essence of it remained, a slash of energy within me, vibrant with power. Perception came from all around me, as if my awareness was suddenly not limited by simple sight or sound. I wasn't made of flesh or teeth anymore, but it didn't matter.

I could still hurt this thing.

The monster howled as I shredded into it. Desperately, it tried to fight me, slashing at me, slicing at my shadowed form. Pain flared like shooting stars wherever it cut, but the sharp agony was distant. Utter rage poured through me, strengthening me, and against that the creature stood no chance.

It spun away, trying to escape me, but it didn't get far. In shards of shadow, it disintegrated, fluttering down in tatters of darkness through the night.

And then there was just me.

Alone in the sky.

With no clue how to stay there.

For one moment, I hovered, all the world spread out beneath me. And then, like Wile E. Coyote when he finally spotted the ground, whatever ability I'd possessed to stay aloft seemed to abandon me.

The forest lurched toward me in fits and starts as I flapped and floundered, but gravity had been beating the shit out of people for millennia and it wasn't about to stop with me. Trees rushed beneath me, coming ever closer. A highway flashed past, and then a river too.

In a shrieking ball of shadow, I tumbled from the sky and splashed into the water. The shock of the cold made whatever power had shifted my form snap me back into human shape again. I narrowly avoided stabbing myself with the blade as I rolled from the impact.

Water soaked my leather gear as I fought to scramble upright against the current. My feet found the bottom only to slip on the slick rocks. Clutching the knife in one hand and paddling frantically with the other, I struggled toward the shore, the heavy clothes weighing me down. My strange night vision oriented me in the darkness where, if I'd still been human, I definitely would have been blind on this moonless night.

My feet found purchase at the edge of the river. The cold gnawed at me, and the dirt of the cemetery had turned to mud on my body. Even shifting shape apparently didn't make that go away. Shivering in my leather coat, I climbed out of the water and started up the wooded slope beyond the shore.

How was I going to get back to the guys? Or back home, for that matter? Someone needed to wake Mom and Dad out of the spell or whatever the hell they were caught in and tell them Harper was dead.

Even if I had no idea how to say that to them.

A sob crushed my chest as I left the tree line and spotted a road ahead. I'd find those creatures. I'd make them pay. I didn't know how, for sure, but I was a vampire now, and I—

Red and blue flashing lights sped around the turn of the road. I stopped, torn on whether to run or shout for help. Surely, these monsters didn't drive cop cars.

Though Mom did.

I froze, silently begging the driver to be my mother. The car veered toward the side of the road quickly, slamming to a halt only a dozen feet away.

The door opened. "Drop the knife!" a man shouted.

I tensed, something in me desperate not to drop Ulysses' blade. But I couldn't even see the cop past the beam of the headlights, and for all I knew, he was pointing a gun at me right now.

Carefully, I lowered the weapon to the concrete.

Beyond the blur of light, I saw a figure move. The gun I'd feared was aimed right at me appeared out of the glare, and when he came close, I winced as he kicked the knife away. Another form followed him, a second cop, her weapon pointed at me as well. I recognized them both from some of the police Christmas parties Mom helped host over the years. "Um, hey, Lieutenant Collins. Sergeant Greenwater. Can you help me—"

"Put your hands behind your back." Lieutenant Collins' voice was like ice.

I floundered. "Put my—"

"You got her?" he snapped to his partner.

"Got her." Sergeant Greenwater's voice was equally cold.

The lieutenant tucked his gun away and spun me around, tugging out his handcuffs as he moved.

"What's going on?" I asked, stumbling as he locked the metal over my wrists.

"You're under arrest for the murder of your sister."

My mouth moved. "W-what? What are you talking about?"

He hauled me around, not answering, and my mind reeled. How could they know about Harper so quickly? I'd only just found her. And the cemetery was overrun by rabids. Had the cops seen the creatures?

What the hell was going on?

"Grab the knife for evidence," he said to his partner, and the woman nodded.

"Evidence?" I sputtered. "I—"

"You have the right to remain silent." He pulled me toward the car. "Anything you say may be used against you in a court of law. You have the right to an attorney. If you cannot afford an attorney..."

I staggered after him, shock leaving me dumbstruck, and when he yanked open the rear door and maneuvered me inside, only one thing came to mind. "I didn't. I swear, I didn't kill her. Please."

He slammed the door in my face.

## 27

ULYSSES

I'd screwed up so much with Wren already.

No way was I going to screw up this.

I sped through the sky, chasing the feeling of my knife in the distance. She'd made it farther than I would have expected, on foot at least. But maybe she'd shifted. Maybe her powers were already growing.

Of course, that might just make her a bigger target.

*Which direction?* Asher sent to me, his words along our bond laced with tension. At his back, Gideon and Liam were closing in fast, barreling through the night sky at a speed that had to be excruciating, considering their weakened state. But I was grateful for it.

Considering we couldn't lose Wren.

*Still west,* I replied. *Moving fast. She—*

Ahead of us, a surge of magic erupted into existence. Invisible against the night sky, it teemed with power like a black hole and crackled against my awareness like an impending lightning strike. I slammed to a halt, shock radiating through me, as the others did the same.

What the hell?

*You fail again, Sentinels.*

The words boomed through my mind like a thunderclap, but the voice wasn't Amalie's. Wasn't anyone I knew. I'd never seen anything like this before in my life, but the sheer *power* coming off it—

A deep chuckle rumbled through my mind. *She's ours now.*

Before I could even move, the wall of magic rushed at us with impossible speed, ripping across our shadow forms. Power scorched over me like fiery acid, stripping away any sense of up or down. Screams filled my head. The dying. The dead. The burned and broken I'd never managed to save. Their hands grabbed for me. Their teeth snapped and snarled, desperate to rip my shadow body to pieces. I thrashed, trying to flee, but they were everywhere. All around me. I couldn't escape, and I—

The feeling vanished, leaving me with air rushing around me, my shadow form gone, and only my utterly human form remaining in the night sky.

And the ground was racing toward me.

I crashed down, smashing through the trees and slamming into the earth below. Pain blasted away my awareness, coating the world in white, only to recede gradually like water soaking into the dirt.

Aching all over, I lay there a moment, taking inventory. Nothing broken, I was fairly certain. Nothing was stabbing my insides, which was good. I gritted my teeth as I pushed away from the ground, my eyes darting over the under-growth for the others. They were still alive; I could feel that. But Liam and Gideon had barely been able to stand before this, and whatever the hell that was couldn't have helped.

And my awareness of my knife was gone.

My breath caught, my own pain fading to distinct second place in my hierarchy of priorities. That... that wasn't possible. Those blades were keyed to our *souls*. I should have been able to find it anywhere on earth. So short of someone destroying the damn thing, there shouldn't have been any way to stop—

"'Lysses?"

Gideon's voice broke into my thoughts, his words slurred. I turned, trying to shift to move faster to reach him, but my body wouldn't change. The power felt drained inside me, and the place where it'd been ached like a raw nerve.

Snarling against the panic that wanted to over-whelm me, I shoved through the bushes and bram-bles to reach him. He lay on his back only inches from a boulder, and he groaned when I moved to help him up. A deep gash marred his forehead, possibly a glancing blow to the massive rock at his side. He must have shifted back too, right before he hit the ground.

Dammit.

"Hang on, man," I muttered to him as I hefted him upright. "I'll get you out of here."

"...the 'ell was that thing?" he grumbled.

"Fuck if I know."

I felt Liam and Asher heading toward us beyond the

small rise in the forest and relief hit me. If they were still standing, then we had a chance to go after her.

Assuming that thing hadn't gotten her first.

I shoved the fear down, my temper flaring. Like hell that invisible thing would take her from us.

Asher shoved a bush aside as he headed toward me, Liam a few steps behind him. "Which way to the knife?"

I bit back a grimace, my determination taking on a sour taste in my mouth.

"Ulysses?"

"It's gone."

Asher stared at me.

"*What?*" Liam demanded.

Gideon mumbled something incoherent, his head lolling. Gods be damned, we needed to get him to Doc Sissoko and fast.

"What, Gideon?" Asher asked.

Gideon sucked down a breath and lurched his head up. "D'that thing do it?"

I glanced between the others. That was a possibility. I could still feel their presences, though, so it wasn't like that creature had—

Asher yanked his knife from its sheath and hurled it at a tree. His head shook. "I can still feel it."

A breath left me. So much for that theory.

"In which direction were you tracking her presence, then?" Asher asked as he made a quick gesture and the knife vanished from the tree trunk.

"West. Maybe another couple miles."

"That puts her in town. She could be anywhere."

I bobbed my head at the obvious and adjusted

Gideon's massive arm on my shoulders. Gods, the man weighed a ton. "Then you better take this guy and get him to the doc while I go after her."

Asher scoffed. "I'm not leaving her—"

"It's my blade. If it reappears, I can track it. But he needs a doctor. Now."

Jaw muscles jumping, Asher regarded me for a moment in silence.

Liam limped between us and gestured sharply. *You both go. I'll get him to the doctor.* Taking Gideon's arm over his shoulders, he glared at us. "And you two better save her."

Without another word, he hefted Gideon's arm into a better position and then took off into the forest, limping with Gideon stumbling along at his side.

I glanced at Asher, finding nothing but resolve in his eyes. I nodded briefly. We'd find her. Wherever she was, we would.

Because like hell I'd screw this up too.

## 28

WREN

"You had a knife, Wren. We got a call about a disturbance at the cemetery. The caller said you and your sister were fighting—*violently*—and when we arrived, we found your sister's body. What more do you want me to say?"

I stared at the detective. His blue eyes were nothing like Liam's. Sharp and hard, they bore into me, already convinced of my guilt, waiting for me to admit it.

"Wren, honey, please. Just tell us why?"

I swallowed hard, unable to meet my mother's pleading gaze. Somehow in the past *however* long it'd been, she'd stopped thinking Harper was on a college trip and switched to some delusion that I'd actually intended to murder my own sister.

If I ever found who'd done this to my family...

I shivered, my cold rage unable to withstand horrible reality. I wasn't some vampire badass. I wasn't even a regular one. And even if I could escape the cuffs, even if I could get out the door, everyone around me was still convinced I was a killer. Beating them up wouldn't change that.

And who was I to argue? If not for me, Harper would still be alive.

My trembling grew worse. I didn't know where the guys were—or even if they'd made it out of the cemetery. Somehow, the cops had known to go there, but they certainly hadn't mentioned seeing amorphous shadow monsters or any of the Sentinels.

No, they'd just been specifically told I was there fighting my sister.

Right before I murdered her.

My eyes flicked to the camera perched high on the wall. Were those government slayer guys behind this? The ones Asher warned me about? Surely those shadow monsters, the rabids, didn't have this kind of power.

Did they?

"You're twenty years old, Wren," the detective said. "You've got your whole life ahead of you. But the judges around here don't exactly have a reputation for being *lenient* when it comes to homicide. Unless you want to spend the rest of your life in prison, you need to open up to us, understand?"

At my silence, he sighed. "Fine." He shoved away from the table. "Can I talk to you outside?"

He directed the words at my mother, who made an agreeing sound and climbed immediately to her feet.

"Think about it, Wren," the detective said when he reached the door. "Anything you say stands a better chance of helping your case than this silence."

I doubted that.

Shaking his head, he held the door for my mother and then followed her outside.

Air escaped me, and I lowered my forehead to my arms, my eyes burning with all the tears I wanted to cry. They had Harper down at the morgue now. For an autopsy, the cops said—not that there was much they seemed to need to determine. Ulysses' knife was their evidence. My fingerprints were obviously all over it, and my sister had a hole in her chest. To the detective, this seemed about as buttoned-up of a case as he'd ever hope to—

Shouts rose beyond the door. Crashing sounds followed, like heavy furniture toppling over, and the impacts made the floor shake. I flinched back as gunfire broke out, peppering the sounds of screaming.

And the noise of guttural growls.

Icy horror raced through my veins. That wasn't the Sentinels. That sounded like the monsters who'd—

The door to the interrogation room crashed down, the hinges and lock clattering to the tile floor. Beyond the opening, snarling people with fangs had overrun the police station. Leaping desks and ripping down officers despite the gunfire aimed at them, the creatures tore through the room and left nothing but death in their wake.

But that wasn't what froze me.

Blood still covering her chest, Harper stood in the doorway.

"Hey, sis." She grinned. "Want to get out of here?"

Thank you for reading Blood
Pawn! Wren and the Sentinels'
story continues in Blood
Captive: Book Two of the
Vampire Rebellion Series.

Want to hear about all Sierra Rowan's stories? Join Sierra's
Insider's Club at sierrarowan.com/subscribe!

# ABOUT THE AUTHOR

Sierra Rowan is the author of action-packed reverse harem paranormal romance and urban fantasy novels. They love to write stories filled with steam, heart, and adventure where a happily-ever-after is guaranteed, even if it takes a few magical battles and car chases to get there.

Get updates about all of Sierra's books at sierrarowan.com.

amazon.com/author/sierrarowan

bookbub.com/authors/sierra-rowan

goodreads.com/sierrarowan

facebook.com/authorsierrarowan

twitter.com/SierraRowanBook

instagram.com/authorsierrarowan

tiktok.com/@sierrarowanbooks